The Life and Times of Alexander Gates

The Life and Times of Alexander Gates

Robert Kelley

To order additional copies of this book, contact:
Xlibris LLC
1-888-795-4274
www.Xlibris.com
Orders@Xlibris.com
142027

Contents

PROLOGUE

My Name Is Alexander Gates

GUESS it would be best to start at the beginning. Otherwise, you – the reader – might get lost. My name is Alexander Gates. When I was two years old, my family got into a terrible car accident. My brother, Jaynes Gates III, told me that our parents gave their lives to assure that we lived. My memories of the event are still fragmented. Even now, I recall flashes of riding in a car seat, in the back of my father's gray sedan. Then a huge red-and-yellow explosion in the middle of an interstate. Lastly, Jaynes holding me in a field in the dead of night, as the car burned in the background. Only in dreams did these memories come. You know how dreams work: some parts are memories, and others are what your mind creates to fill the void.

After that, my brother and I went to a town outside Buffalo, New York, to live with my grandfather, Jaynes Gates Sr. My grandfather owned seventy acres of land on which he lived in a large three-story home. He was a carpenter by trade and had designed the place from the ground up. He told Jaynes and me that he made it as a gift to our grandmother. A high metal fence surrounded the property, with a long driveway that led up to the house. The front yard had a few lawn gnomes, a bird feeder, and a plastic pink flamingo. The hardwood porch had four steps that led to it, and the foundation featured glass block windows that protected the basement. The roof looked normal for the ladder nailed to it. Why it was there, I never knew, but it was one of the many oddities our home contained.

Walking through the living room, random boards would creak as you stepped. We had them memorized so that we could sneak out in the middle of the night. There were brown curtains hanging on over windows that matched a couch set that he still had before Grandma passed away. Just beyond the sitting area was a dining room. It had a glass dinner table with four light brown wooden chairs. A display cabinet stood to the right of the table that held a few small knives, some lighters, and something that looked like a glass eye. On its top shelf, there was a photo album, opened to a black-and-white picture of my grandparents' wedding day. He was wearing a black tux, and Grandma had a white dress with a bouquet of flowers clutched in her hand. At the far end of the room was a doorway leading into a kitchen.

The inside was typical as far as kitchens go. It had a stove on your right side as you entered. The refrigerator that stood next to it was black with an ice dispenser on its freezer door. A large stainless-steel sink on the far wall had a counter that extended to the back doorway. This door concealed a set of steps on the right. They were attached to the side wall leading upstairs. Another door on the left marked the basement. The stairs led up into a long hallway. The first room to the right was mine. I had lost many hours educating myself in the ways of women, amateur chemistry, and all the insurmountable lives wasted in games like Halo and Baldur's Gate.

Across from my room was Jaynes's. Further down was a bathroom – the only one we used in such a big home. Just farther still was another set of rooms placed across from each other. They were used as guest rooms when company visited. At the end was a narrow staircase, up to which led to Grandpa's private study and bedroom.

Grandpa dressed like a board member of some large business, wearing shiny shoes and tan pants with a nice button-up shirt. His eyes were hazel, his hair black with a streak of gray running across the right side of his head. His mustache was usually shaven down to his smooth tan skin. He would leave a small patch of gray fuzz upper lip. A line of buzzed hair from one sideburn to the other would create his beard.

Growing up, it was just us three: Grandpa, Jaynes, and I. Grandpa's motto was "If you do something positive, it will come back to you tenfold. If you do something negative, it will also come back tenfold. Two sides to the same coin." He was good at telling stories. If he wasn't making up stories about magic, it was his adventures from the two wars he served in. There was always something to learn when Grandpa spoke. He even had us working in a food kitchen to teach us humility.

Jaynes, who preferred a more urban look, wore jeans with a white tee shirt. His light brown eyes would always get compliments. I don't know what it is about boys with long hair, but most girls loved Jaynes. His hair was usually combed back into a long tail he'd been growing ever since the accident, in honor of our parents. I recall when he was in seventh grade, Cali Brown proclaimed she was his girlfriend. She ran around school screaming it to whoever would listen. Jaynes just went along because he really didn't want to hurt her feelings. They dated for a year and then she moved away because her parents got a new job somewhere in the Midwest.

Jaynes and I had the typical brotherhood relationship. He seemed to have all the coolest things, and of course, he would never let me touch them. Come to think of it, there were a lot of off-limits back then. That was because Grandpa liked his privacy. His study and bedroom on the third floor – we were not allowed in. Also, there was the basement, the door of which was always padlocked. Access was never granted to us.

Once, Jaynes tried to pick it. Grandpa had left to go to a Renaissance fair. So after he had left, Jaynes brings out a set of lock picks that he'd bought from a magazine, and together, we went to the door. I was in back while Jaynes stood in front. The lock hung in its place, nonverbally taunting us into doing the deed. Jaynes walked up and grasped it in his right palm. The first pick he inserted into the keyhole got stuck in a gear, so he took out another to remove the first. Suddenly, we heard the sound of metal scraping, then an ear-splitting crack. The second lock pick he was using had broken. The first stood vibrating in the keyhole.

The mistake of my life is when I said "You suck at lock-picking!" His face quickly contorted itself. Jaynes chased me up to the second floor. Just before I made it to my room, he grabbed me by the rim of my collar and shoved me into the broom closet. A click announced to me that he had locked the door. At first, the darkness wasn't bad, but as time rolled on, panic consumed me. My fists tightened as I banged for at least two hours. Then I slumped into a pile of old boxes and fell into despair.

The thought that Grandpa wouldn't be home until the morning slowly became apparent. Later, I heard the lock click open, then light footsteps. Quickly I reached for the doorknob and jumped out into an empty hallway. Fresh footprints in the rug led to Jaynes's room. Figuring he must have felt bad, I went into my room, closing the door behind me. Jaynes was always worrying about others. He would try to protect them from things. I guess it shouldn't have surprised me when he left for basic training. He had joined the military after high school. At his going-away party, Grandpa gave a speech about how he had great pride for Jaynes fighting for our country.

Around the neighborhood, Grandpa was viewed as eccentric but still managed to be well liked. Every now and then, he'd give a pool party for all our neighbors. Everyone would come and bring dishes to share. I remember Grandpa met his girlfriend at one of these gatherings. Mrs. Gloria Caldaria – she came wearing a pink two-piece bathing suit. When she came into our backyard, Mr. Brown choked on his martini. Mr. Benjamin had to pat him on his back to get him to stop. Her toenails, which gleamed through her open-toed sandals, matched her outfit. Her youthful look did not foretell her age.

Grandpa had all types of weird ornaments from his travels, most of which were displayed all over the house. Mayan masks, suits of armor and weapons from all around the world. Oh yeah, and his pride and joy: a Gypsy shaman's staff. He did other things too, like hang garlic, bushes of clovers, iron horseshoes, and jade around the house. According to him, it's to keep the house lucky. The oddest thing of all was whenever he would have company. They were always quickly swept into the basement. That would be the last we'd see of them for the rest of the night. Sometimes, on the next morning, the guest-room doors would be closed. When we came home later, for the most part they would be gone. Once in a blue moon, they might stay the day till the next night.

Grandpa was what most people would call a neat freak, constantly cleaning. Our house had the aroma of fresh pine; it would overwhelm your senses as you came through the front door. The wax shine could blind you as it beamed off the wood planks that composed the floor. Everything was to be spotless, or else a large vein would pop out of his neck while he calmly gave us orders.

CHAPTER 1

The Return

THE last time I had seen Grandpa alive was at my college graduation; he was eighty-four at the time. After the ceremony, he took me to the side slightly away from everyone. I thought he would give me some family heirloom, but instead, he told me he was very proud of me, and that nothing I do from that point on could make him prouder. Also, that I had obtained knowledge. Now I needed to find patience to maintain myself and not let darkness take hold in my heart. Then he took both of my hands and drew two ruins on my palms. He looked into my eyes and smiled. When he released me, I noticed the ink marks had disappeared. Brushing it out of my mind, we joined a congregation of people celebrating our graduation. Afterward Jaynes, I, Grandpa, and Mrs. Caldaria went out to dinner. A week later, he passed away.

Jaynes and I had to make most of the preparations for his funeral. The service was full of faces of which few I was familiar with. More than a thousand people showed up. It was at that point I realized I knew very little about the man who was my only guardian. Being the eldest, Jaynes was presented with a folded triangular flag along with "the deepest condolences for our loss." As one hundred Marines did their rifle salute, I noticed a chill run through the crowed. As each shot rang, some of the members of those gathered winced as if they had received a bullet themselves. We stood there like the good sons he raised us to be.

Person after person came to us to shake our hands in an attempt to console us in our time of grieving. Mrs. Caldaria took us both in her arms and whispered,

"If you need anything, don't hesitate to ask. I'm hurting also. We are together in all of this." Then she kissed us and left.

The procession filed out in a slow pace, some stopping at the casket to say their thoughts for the last time. There was one teenage kid who was crying so hard, he just plowed through the line and disappeared into the headstones.

A week after the funeral, a lawyer called Jaynes and me into his office to read Grandpa's will. To Mrs. Caldaria, he left an undisclosed amount of money and a letter. Most of the objects were given to a few of his friends, but to us, he left an assortment of keys on an antique ring and our childhood home. Jaynes having a house of his own, my grandfather gave it to me.

The day after the reading, I went to check out the building that I hadn't been to in years. Slowly, I opened the door; it creaked lightly then gave way to the darkness inside. My first step inside was marked in the layer of dust on the floor. It looked as if it hadn't been occupied in years. There were white sheets on all of the furniture. It appeared that spiders were the only residents for three years. You could tell by the intricate webbing across the ceiling. Out of habit, I went to work cleaning. By the time I had finished, the night had enveloped the town. I curled up in my old room and stared at the glow of the decals planets starting to peel off the ceiling. I lay there for a while thinking of how long it had been since I had returned. Slowly sleep crept into my eyes, causing my snores to echo through the house.

Suddenly, a loud thud woke me from a deep slumber. There was someone moving around downstairs. So I jumped out of the bed and grabbed the twelve-gauge from the gun case in the hall. Slowly I crept down the stairs to the empty kitchen. When I entered the dining room, a man was going through our grandfather's display cabinet. When he heard the click as I cocked the gun back, he spun around, eyes as large as dinner plates. Dropping to his knees, he shuddered. "Please don't shoot me. I am a friend of your grandfather Zavies. You can call me K'Shan."

I looked at him carefully, dazed and confused. He was just short of five feet tall. He had orange hair and green eyes. What I thought was a jacket was actually a traveling cape with a green hood. I tightened my grip on the gun. I then said, "First off, my grandfather's name was Jaynes. Second, what are you doing in my house?"

He started to shake uncontrollably, his eyes rolled into the back of his head, and then he passed out. I picked him up, laid him on the couch, and called the police. They arrived in thirty minutes, just like a pizza man on a deadline. They questioned me on what happened, collected the deranged man, then left.

Alone with my thoughts, curiosity crept over me. What exactly was in the house that would cause a crazy old man to break in? I combed the house looking for some hint of what he would be looking for. I checked every nook and cranny for clues. Then to be on the safe side, I thought I'd better rummage through

Grandpa's room. Stepping in the study, it had a soft green carpet that covered the whole floor. The walls were lined with bookshelves full of miscellaneous texts. Some scrolls were stuffed into what looked like a wine rack in a corner. There was a large desk in the middle of the room that faced the entrance. It was stacked with piles of dusty books, a couple of old feathers placed in an ink bottle, a few pens, and some pencils scattered across its top. There was a stained glass window set to the left of the desk with a picture of the Last Supper on it.

I crossed the room to an archway behind the desk. Upon entering the medium-sized space, I noticed a bed placed against the far wall in such a way that one could get out of bed on either side. There was a nightstand with a half-burned white candle on top. Wax had drizzled down the holder to harden on the oak surface. A dresser placed on the right side of the bed had a jewelry box on it. I figured whatever that thief wanted was inside of it. So I walked over and tried to open it. "Locked," I muttered. It was then I remembered the set of keys my grandfather had given me.

I ran to my room and grabbed the ring of keys out of my bag. Running as the sweat dripped off my forehead, I dashed back upstairs to my treasure chest. In haste, I tripped over the chair and fell. The keys flew out of my hands and slid under the bed. I crawled over to the bed and felt into the darkness underneath. The dust bunnies were sent running till my hand ran over the cold round metal. I grasped the ring, stood up, then walked over to the dresser. I placed the keys in the lock one after another until, at last, the box gave a small click. My anticipation bubbled over as the top flipped open. Then, all too quickly, my dreams were crushed. It was filled to the top with different-colored glass stones, the same ones you see in beta fishbowls. In complete disappointment, I went back to the study. I flopped in a beanbag chair near the window and peered out into the darkness.

I spent the rest of the night in the study going through all of the texts, figuring that I was already here. There were all types of books. First I pulled out a book called *Magic in Cooking*. It had funny rhymes about cooking all types of food. There was another one called *True History of the World*. Supposedly, magical folks and humans lived together on this planet for all of our history. It really seemed like a history book except it intertwined truth with magical fiction. It stated that most human cities were built with the help of dwarfs. Humans lived in harmony with magic as we evolved.

I flipped ahead and found an article about the Middle Ages. It said how humans turned their backs on magic, choosing to persecute those who kept these types of relations. Whether relations were benign or malevolent, it didn't matter. In the eyes of those in power, to know magic was a reason to be put to death. This enraged a bulk of the magical community, creating a rift that ultimately caused magic folk to leave the realm. Very few stayed here, and those that did formed secret communities in hope that, one day, humans would see the error in their ways.

Pieces of information made me curious. Like where are the places that these so-called magic people live in? I was pretty decent at history in school, so I knew that most of the stories in these books were false. So as far as I knew, humans have searched most of the world and found no sign of magic. I kept flipping through the book for some time and then the phone rang. The sudden noise startled me so that I dropped the book. I dashed over to pick up the phone. On the other line was my girlfriend Ontia. I had met her in my Anatomy class back in college; it was one of the night classes I had in my freshman year. We spoke briefly on the phone, and then afterward, I went back up to the book.

As I bent down to pick it up, I noticed an old piece of paper that had fallen out onto the floor. I picked it up and flattened it on top of the desk. Written on it was a riddle, "Only when your mind is open to new possibilities can you traverse the waters as though they were a highway. Show us your truest virtues. Only then shall the road to Subterra open to you." Just as I started to ponder the cryptic message, the doorbell rang.

I ran downstairs and opened the door, and in stepped the most beautiful visage I had ever beheld. Long flowing dark hair – skin pale enough that if you were to shine a light on her, one would think she'd turn red. Her eyes so green that even the foliage got jealous as she passed. She floated through the doorway as if on air. Every curve magnified by a thin strapped black dress trimmed in silver. Losing sight of her, I turned to close the door. As I spun, she advanced forward tucking her hair behind her ear and softly kissing me on my lips. So drawn to her, I failed to notice myself encircled by her arms. How entranced was I that when I regained my senses, we were lying in the bed just before the sun awoke. How I got there was a blur of images – none of which were in any order.

She lay next to me sound asleep, her chest falling slightly as she dreamed away. The curtains were drawn close so that not a drop of light filtered through. In the darkness, I crept out of bed, trying not to disturb her slumber. Down the hall and up the stairs, I went into the study. The questions of the night before clear in my head, I paged through tome after tome. A new mission burned into my mind: what is Subterra? Ripping through line after line, the concept of time fell away. All around me, the world came alive. The sun beamed through a stained-glass window, creating a rainbow across the floor. Just beyond, squirrels scurried back and forth as though trying to break in, although such thoughts were lost in my meticulous screening. Just as I finished tossing a book entitled *Magical People in Western New York* aside, Ontia came up the stairs carrying a plate topped with blueberry pancakes. Clutched in the other hand was a large mug of coffee.

Demanding I stop for a break, she inquired as to my objectives in such a frivolous search. After gathering an appropriate answer, she stopped and sat down. As I finished consuming the delicious breakfast she prepared, Ontia inquired if my grandfather kept a journal or diary of some kind. I thought for a while then said, "To my knowledge, he didn't." But when I turned for a superficial look at the room, there it was, sitting on top of the stack nearest to me – as if it knew I was looking for it. I picked it up and flipped to the first page. The first chapter was called "Subterra – The Home of the Elder Race." It told of a city that glows deep beneath the Earth. There was only one way to reach the city, which was to obtain two magical relics of old. The first was to be found in a great forest. The second was to be revealed once the other was found by their master.

I glanced at Ontia, toying with the notion that this place might actually be real. "What did it say?" she asked. The air of mild curiosity ran across her face.

Then I thought, *How crazy would she think me if I repeated the things in this book?* Quickly I made up a lie and said, "It was about a trip around the world that Grandpa had taken when he was younger."

She smiled once again and cleaned up the dishes. Then she went downstairs to watch TV. Left alone, the thought of a magical place being somewhere torched the inside of my mind. I never knew my grandfather to lie to me, but these stories in a so-called diary could not possibly be true. He had many works of fiction on his shelves. Could this not be his attempt to create his own? If so, why write it in a journal? Finding this thing caused me to have more questions than answers.

The only person I felt comfortable telling this to would be Jaynes. I was not surprised when he said I was crazy the next day. I told him everything that had happened the night before.

He sat for a while, pondering what I had just explained. Then he smiled and said, "You are feeding into Grandpa's illusion that he was somehow magic-born. Yeah, he told me those stories when I was little. You and I both know that Elfin folk or even fairies do not exist. I really need to get you away from here. The stress of losing Grandpa has taken a toll on your mind. You know I was going to go camping to relax next week. Maybe you and Ontia would like to join me. It is possible that Grandpa just wrote those stories in the hope that they would be published. So let's just go somewhere we can kick back and enjoy the nature."

CHAPTER 2

The Trip

M E, Jaynes, Ontia, and her friend Nevalin decide to go to Allegany State Park so Jaynes wouldn't be alone. Ontia knew Nevalin from grade school. She was a runway model and had done commercials for *Cover Girl*, *Victoria's Secret*, and a few others. Ontia and I sat in the front, while Jaynes and Nevalin sat in the back trying to get to know each other. He seemed to be content to rub her feet while she talked about all the people she knew. I sat in the passenger seat staring at the farms fly past as we drove across the countryside. Cows and sheep grazed in the fields, while old equipment was left to rust in the barns. Over rolling hills and across a few bridges we went, down to the border were New York met Pennsylvania. Until a large sign announced to us we had arrived at our destination.

We pulled up at a large structure with a sign on it that said Red House. We got out and entered the building. We stepped into a hallway with a hardwood counter. The attendant handed us our cabin keys, and we went into a gift shop. There was a stuffed bear with a hat placed on his head. I and Jaynes took turns putting our hands in its mouth or acting as if we were being mauled; the girls browsed the shop for souvenirs. We headed out and passed a great lake with an island placed in the middle. Driving down roads that entered the forest, we came to a trail off the main road which led to a small clearing with cabins spaced apart from each other. I could see kids running around playing as their families sat relaxing on the porch of their cabins. Our cabin was set in a thicket of trees. There was a community bathroom/shower of which Ontia complained loudly.

"Well, at least we have electricity," Nevalin said in a compromising tone.

As the others unpacked, I examined the surroundings. The cabin was located with a stream just alongside it. The cabin itself was quite like the other cabins. There was a hardwood porch, with a screen door propped open by a large rock. The inside door had to be unlocked with a key. Entering it, I noticed there were four cots stacked on top of each other to save space. There was an electric heater next to the wall. In a small corner, there was an old cast-iron wood-burning stove with an electric one next to that. We took the cots from atop one another. We placed mine and Ontia's side by side. Nevalin was situated so that no sun reached her, whether it was day or night. Jaynes placed his next to hers, being careful to leave a sufficient space to walk in between them. There was a painted wood table with two identical benches stacked on top of it. We dragged it out onto the porch to the railing, which was the ideal spot to lounge.

Nevalin presented the idea to go on a nature walk. Jaynes jumped at the chance to be alone with her and said, "I'll go." But when Ontia injected with "Let's walk on one of those trails we passed on the way in," Jaynes's face went from a smile to a grimace in less than a heartbeat.

"I am going to stay here, you guys go have fun." As the words passed my lips, a big frown spread across Ontia's face. "You and I can go for a walk alone later," I responded. So as Ontia, Nevalin, and Jaynes departed – leaving me to my own contemplations – I grabbed my bag and pulled out the diary. Looking through the book's many entries, I came to an excerpt entitled "The Great Forest."

It started out explaining how the forest stretches from the eastern ocean through to where the ground turns firm with small shrubs and grassy knolls. How a mountain range ran from the northern ice fields, where the long-tooth mammals reigned to the south near to where the top of Florida is now. There was a symbol that resembled a gathering of enormous boulders that were left over from the great iceberg migration. I turned the page to find a map of what looked like North America. Close to the border of Pennsylvania would be where the large rocks were. In comparing the diary to a map I picked up in the gift shop, it looked as if the rocks were congregated in a spot labeled Thunder Rock, which was located in the park. Then I heard the sound of Ontia and Nevalin chatting loudly as the gravel crunched under their feet. Quickly I stored the diary under my sleeping bag and went out of the cabin to greet them.

The first person I saw was Jaynes with the sourest look on his face. He walked past me into the cabin. I heard him say under his breath, "I wish you would have kept her at the cabin." As the door slammed closed, the girls walked up the creaky wooden stairs and sat at the table. They started to tell me about seeing a fox on the way back.

"He was so cute with his little fluffy tail and pointed nose," Nevalin squealed.

"Yeah, and he had orange-and-black fur," excitedly responded Ontia.

Then we heard Jaynes rumbling around inside the cabin. Ontia looked at me and said, "Your brother is so stupid. He did not even talk to Nevalin."

A smirk spread across my face as I responded, "He originally thought they were going alone."

The sun gave way, letting the moon take its place in the sky. We gathered a bunch of wood to start a fire. Of course, it was I who was delegated to start it. The fire pit was lined with large river stones that formed a circle. First, I cleared the pit of debris that had not burned from a previous fire. Then I carefully arranged some stones to make a tighter circle to keep the flames contained. After everything was in place, I took a large page from an old newspaper we found inside and crumpled it up into a tight ball. Then I took a few small dry twigs and set them on top of the newspaper. I stood up to admire my work. It wasn't much, but I made it work. Retrieving a lighter from my back pocket (I never leave home without one), I attempted to start it. At first, the paper would not stay lit. So I took a few scraps of wood we had brought with us and placed them around the paper to stop the wind from knocking it away. Soon, the fire was burning hot and bright. Sitting close, you could feel the heat sear your face as if it was cooking your skin. The embers floated up into the sky as the blaze consumed the rest of the original paper. Periodically, we added more wood to keep the fire from going out.

"Hey, I got an idea. Let's go look at this tomorrow," I spoke as I pointed at the spot on the gift shop map where the boulders were.

"Yeah, we can go – as long as you are coming." As he spoke, spit flew from Jaynes's mouth. It landed softly on my lip.

Wiping my mouth with disgust, I said, "I'll take a shower in the morning, thank you."

Nevalin chuckled quietly in her chair. Jaynes stood up quickly, making Ontia say, "Boys, boys, we came out here to relax. Stop your bickering." She put her hand on Jaynes's shoulder as he slid back into his chair slowly.

Nevalin changed the subject of conversation. "Do you guys think the Earth is dying? You know – global warming and all."

"That's a morbid outlook on it," I responded.

"No, that's a good way of looking at it," said Ontia.

"Now why is that? I understand the oceans are heating up. Rivers are receding. Parts of the world are having harsh weather patterns, but how can the Earth die?" I said.

Jaynes opened his mouth to say something, but Nevalin interrupted, "If you compare the world to a human, they are the same. The veins of the Earth are the rivers. The skin is stone. The organs are lakes and oceans. Humans purify food by digestion, the Earth by its many processes."

"Wow, you basically read my mind," Jaynes said with a slightly nostalgic look on his face. He smiled and sat back away from the fire. "I guess in that way of thinking – then yes, one could say it was dying."

I gave in. Ontia then broke out a large bottle of red wine for herself and Nevalin, spending the rest of the time passing it back and forth. I pulled out a bottle of vodka. When all that was left of our fire was small smoking embers of a log, we noticed our bottles were empty. Jaynes and I stumbled to the cabin and passed out. Sometime later, I felt Ontia's cold body snuggle close and pull the blankets up. By the time our bodies were warm, the sun had brought the dawn's rays of light.

It wasn't until noon when a horn from the neighbors' truck shook the door; only then did I wake. Ontia had the blankets pulled over her head, as did Nevalin. Jaynes was sprawled across his cot, blankets thrown to the floor. Masked by his snores, I crept through the cabin. Outside, I sat on the bench and rested my arms on the table. I watched a squirrel climb up a tree to a branch out of view. Deer were grazing on the wet grass in a field across the way. I stretched out and laid my head on the railing, wrapping around the porch.

All at once, a feeling came over me – one I hadn't felt in a long time. Peace, it seemed like the only things awake with me were the animals. The whole park was calm. I closed my eyes for a minute or two, and then the sound of running came from behind the cabin. As swiftly as possible, I got up and dashed around the cabin. Off in the distance, I saw what looked like a deer, but it was too far away to make it out clearly. I walked back to the front of the structure slowly. I picked up a long stick and took it up to the porch. I brought out my knife and started to make myself a walking stick. By the time I was finished, Jaynes had woken up – which was around midafternoon. Jaynes made the suggestion that we leave the girls and go to the rocks by ourselves. Considering how late they were up, I decided it was a good idea. So I snuck back in the cabin, grabbed the keys, two premade subs, and left the girls snoring away.

We drove to the other side of the park. Pulling up, I saw that we were not the only people that wanted to see the huge boulders. Other vehicles were parked in scattered positions. We stepped out onto the stony ground as another car pulled up. Kids darted up the path lined by thin, tall trees. The leaves above created somewhat of a canopy, similar to that of a rainforest. Light cascaded down, kissing the forest floor in spots, giving it the effect of a human-sized chessboard. Children darted to and fro, some climbing the large rocks. Others ran here or there, playing tag in the shadows of these giants. We walked deeper through the grass, to a large stone set kind of away from the others.

At some point, our stomachs told us it was time to eat. So we sat in the shadow of this mammoth piece of stone. Pulling out the subs, we started to eat. My chicken-finger sub was so filling that I took half and wrapped it up for later. I set it on top of my bag and stood up to stretch. Then I turned to look at Jaynes while he finished the last of his Philly steak hoagie. A gust of wind a propelled white plastic bag past; I watched it float away caught in its eternal breath. A gaggle of teens tramped by, talking loudly about a deer they were trying to track. Then I turned to my sandwich, but it was not there. Figuring I forgot I put it in my bag, I started to scrounge inside. Not there either, I turned to Jaynes and said, "Stop playing games and give me my half a sub back."

He looked up with a bewildered look then responded with "I'm full off of my own hoagie. Why would I eat yours?"

"Well, if you didn't eat it, then where is it?" I responded.

Sitting on his brick rocking backing forth, Jaynes let out a mocking howl of laughter. "If you are too stupid to keep track of your own food, that's not my problem," he murmured in between fits of snickering.

Walking over, I snatched up his bag and started to search the inside. Jaynes jumped up and smacked the bag from my hand to the ground. "DON'T TOUCH MY STUFF!" he screamed. "What is wrong with you? I said I didn't take your food," Jaynes said angrily.

Then suddenly, I heard someone giggling loudly nearby. Sprinting around the whole boulder, I returned to Jaynes out of breath. Not finding anyone, I questioned Jaynes, "Did you hear someone laughing?"

He responded with a shake of the head to say yes. "Maybe there's someone on top," Jaynes interjected.

So I searched around to find a way to climb up. After circling another two times, I stopped to catch my breath. Feeling a pain in my side, I reached my right hand out to steady myself on the boulder. But instead of a solid surface, my arm just slid through the stone. My first instinct was to pull myself free, but the harder I pulled, the more I was sucked in. It felt as though my whole arm was entrapped by quicksand. Faster and faster it reeled me in with its gritty grip, until it was not only my arm that was trapped but half of my body as well. So before my head was submerged, I screamed for Jaynes.

The sound of his footsteps told me that he was running to me, but when he got into view, all he was only able to glimpse was my head before it disappeared into the stone. I shut my eyes tightly and held my breath, thinking death was moments away. Just inches from my face, I could hear Jaynes calling out to me, but I could not respond back. One minute later, I felt the feeling of wet sand go away as I fell onto a wooden planked floor. At once, everything was quiet except for what sounded like the daily news – but how? I was so far away from civilization that the thought of a television sounded absurd. I opened my eyes to try and see where I was. In doing so, what I witnessed caused me to question my sanity.

CHAPTER 3

The First Introduction

I LAY in the doorway of a large cabin; a shield gleamed down on me from atop the door. As I rolled over onto my hands, I was able to view the rest of the first floor. The TV room had a love seat, an armchair, and sofa – all with a light floral pattern. There was a big area rug underneath all of the furniture. The rug's pattern was of leaves and flowers made of blue, black, green, and some burgundy. There was white silk weaved in as highlights. It had a beautifying effect on the bare walls. Near the stairway leading to the second floor, there as an oriental vase sitting on a large curled leaf made of iron. After standing, I turned to open the front door. But when I did, all that was beyond the frame was a sheer solid surface. I put my ear to it, feeling the cold and hard stone. No sound entered into my eardrum. Then I heard the sound of movement from the second floor. Panicking, I dove into the front room and hid behind the sofa, just out of sight of the wooden stairway. My heart pounded in time with the footsteps of the resident of this domicile as it walked down the steps in a slow pace. Coming down the stairs was a thin man with hair that fell down to his bottom jaw. The hair hung in layers like sheets of orange silk. His tattered clothing looked as if it had been scrounged together. He walked over to the door, closing it. Then he turned around and looked over the house. As his eyes scanned the front room, I ducked my head back behind the sofa's arm.

Then I heard the same laugh as I had outside. A voice rang out and said, "I know there is someone in my house. Who's there? Come out now and I won't turn you into something horrible."

Fear held me in place. One: I had broken into someone's house. Two: whomever this person was that lived in a rock was threatening me with dismemberment.

The man let out another cackling laugh, then pointed to the couch and started to whisper. At once, the sofa floated into the air, leaving me exposed. "There you are," the male spoke with enthusiasm. The couch settled back down on the ground as the man took a seat in the armchair. "Come out, you have already been found. So no more hide-and-seek, as fun a game as it may be," he said as he sat in the armchair, picking his slightly tan nose. Coming out, I sat across from him on the couch, trying to speak, but the words of my voice gummed up my throat, like too much peanut butter.

Taking advantage of my bewilderment, he said, "You look like someone I knew a long time ago, although I can't place the nose. Anyway, welcome. My name is Lamel. Lamel Laymaine." He bent down and took a piece of toffee off the table. Unwrapping it, he tossed it into his mouth. He spoke again, but this time he had a smile that stretched across his face. "So how is it that you come to be in my sitting room hiding behind that moth-eaten couch?"

The words tumbled out of my mouth before I had a chance to think them through! "I came to this park because my grandfather said I might find Subterra. How I fell through that rock, I have no clue. I just touched it and got sucked in."

The look on Lamel's face went from cheerful to one of a questioning air. "Sucked in, you say. Here is an easy one – who is your grandfather to know that place? I mean you're clearly human, so there can be no way you know it," he demanded.

Feeling offended, I stood on my feet.

"Where are you going? You can't leave yet, we've only just met," he spoke in a kind voice as he stood as well.

"Did you take my food?" I said as I folded my arms.

"And it was very good, thanking you, but didn't you give it to me? I mean to say, it was just sitting on my windowsill and I was just so hungry at the moment." Lamel answered as if he were making a fact.

"Dude, are you being serous right now? It looks like a giant boulder on the outside. How could anyone have known it was your house!" I was waving my arms as I spoke.

"With this!" he said as he pointed to his left hand.

There on his index finger was a gold ring. Atop it was a jade stone encrusted by a symbol made of small glittering fragments that reflected white.

"What is it?" I asked as he sat back down in the chair and started to smile once again.

"A gift from my mother, but she doesn't live here anymore. Anyway, you never told me your name," he said.

"Alexander Gates, but that's beside the point. How could that ring let me see your house on the outside?" I said.

"Come on, Lexxy, you have come all this way and you don't know about magic?" he said in a mocking tone.

"Don't call me that. I hate it when Jaynes says that. Oh my god. He's outside thinking I died." I was speaking in a panicking tone.

Lamel spoke calmly. "He left saying something about going crazy, as you were looking around my house. I just figured out who you look like!"

"What? What are you talking about?" I said, dazed by his unorganized questions.

"Remember, I said you look familiar. I just figured out who it was," he said, laughing hard in the chair.

"Who do I look like?" I spoke.

"This old guy that used to hang around my mom – Zavies I think his name was," he said, taking another piece of toffee and eating it.

There is that name again, I thought to myself. Fishing for more information, I asked, "So what did he and your mom do together?"

"Nothing much, this was when I was younger than you. I think he was some family member, but I don't recall clearly. It's been many years since then," he answered. "So what is your grandfather's name?" he asked again.

"Jaynes Gates," I said proudly.

"I'm truly sorry for your loss," he said, pointing at a stack of newspapers.

I walked over and, a few papers down, I found an article about Grandpa's funeral. Suddenly, a vision flashed in my head of the line of people who shook my hand at the end of the burial. "You were there, weren't you? You broke through the line at the end?" I asked in a low tone.

He lowered his head and said, "Yeah, I don't like graveyards. They're too full of endings."

"Why were you there?" I questioned out loud.

"Well, my mom made me. She told me it would be the least I could do. They were on the council together," he said. "She told me that he was one of the guardians of our two realms," he continued.

"So Subterra does exist!" I proclaimed.

"Wait, I never said that. You didn't here that from me," he said in defense.

"No, but you did say that there is a council. And where would a council preside but in a city," I said out loud while putting it together in my head.

"Enough of this mess. Let me see your hands," he said in final tone.

I looked down at my hands. Except for some dirt smudges, they looked normal. So I held them out palms up for him to inspect. When he saw them, his eyes widened so big that the pupils overtook the whites. Hands shaking, he stepped back muttering, "You are the one, the markings don't lie! You are the one!"

I tried to touch him, but he withdrew from my reach. "No, it's not time yet. It can't be. Something is wrong – something is horrible wrong," he said.

Lamel turned and ran upstairs. In curiosity, I followed him. The second floor was very unusually big. There were twelve rooms down a long hallway, six on each side, with a picture on the walls between each room. At the end of the hall, there was a metal spiraling staircase leading to a third floor. I started up the corridor toward the staircase. The pictures were of the same landscape, but different shots. It gave me the effect of walking through the countryside. When I reached the end, Lamel was coming down the stairs. He was carrying a large purple book. The cover had a metal lion's head embroidered into it.

He smiled at me and walked over, saying, "I am sorry for my reaction. Your presence here surprised me."

I responded with "I've been here for a while now. You're not making sense to me."

"This book will explain everything. I must prepare for what is to come. It was very nice to meet you, and I hope to see you again. Be safe," Lamel spoke as he put the book in a bag. Handing me the bag, he then led me back downstairs. He then opened the front door and waved his arm as if to show me the way out.

"This is all fine and dandy, but how am I supposed to leave? There is a great slab of rock blocking my way," I said.

Lamel slapped his forehead saying, "I forgot. Here, take this back. It has always been yours – or so I'm told." He handed me his ring. When I took it, he said, "Put it on and you will see the truth."

So I shrugged and slid it on my right ring finger. With a flash of light, the rock that was blocking my way out vanished. It was replaced by a brown welcome mat with green leaves spelling out the word. I looked back at Lamel, and he waved his hand again. I grabbed his hand and shook it lightly, then left. Outside, I turned around to look at the rock, but it had been replaced with large three-story gray stone mansion.

There were windows placed at intervals around the first floor. I could actually see the fireplace through one of the glass panes. There was even a planter that I didn't notice before. I turned around and started to walk down the path leading to where we parked the car. The time spent with Lamel allowed the night to creep upon me. I quietly stepped in-between the boulders that marked the way through the darkness. All the cars had left by the time I reached the small river stones that made the parking lot. So I started to make the long hike through the dense forest. Fireflies flickered their light just ahead of me as if leading the way. After a while, my eyes adjusted to the limited light of the stars twinkling high above.

Then as if from nowhere, a large mass came bounding through the stillness of the forest. It collided into my back, throwing me to the ground. The bag I was carrying flew out of my hand into the brush. I and the other body hit the ground, rolling in the dirt. Dust kicked up into the air as we tumbled down the road along the hill. My muffled cries of pain went unheard in the darkness. When I reached the bottom of the hill, my body collided with the side of a parked car. Then a voice came from above me, "You are such a fuckoff! Move your ass!"

Jaynes pushed me from atop. He started screaming, "Where did you go? I figure that you were hiding somewhere around! So I left screaming I was going to get the girls! If you ever do that to me again, I'll kill you."

I stood there feeling two feet tall. Then I said, "Where are the girls?"

He smacked me in the head and pointed to the car I collided into previously. There, sitting in the front seats, were Ontia and Nevalin chatting calmly to one another. Before Jaynes and I piled in and headed to the cabin, I scanned the area for what knocked me down the hill but didn't see anything.

CHAPTER 4

The Next Day

I CHECKED the time when we reached the campsite. The radio display gleamed 2:30 a.m. in a green light from the dashboard. Jaynes parked the car and got, out slamming the door behind him.

Nevalin reached over the seat, laying her hand on my shoulder. "He was really worried about you." When she spoke, her words came in an odd tone – as if she was holding back something – then removed her hand and got out of the car as well.

Ontia leaned over and kissed me then lay back. When she smiled, her teeth shined in the moonlight. Her eyes were so wide they looked almost black for a moment. As her blinking brought me back to reality, she spoke in a lighthearted manner, "So, baby, did you have fun scaring me to death?" She giggled to herself then said, "Did you bring me anything back?"

For the first time that morning, I smiled. Then I said "I'll tell you later" and leaned in and kissed her again. We slept the rest of the morning in the car.

The sun woke me by beaming into my eye through the windshield. Ontia was snuggled up next to me, hidden in the shade. I slid out of the car trying not to wake her. There were still a few red coals in the fire pit turning to ash gray. I walked over to the porch and thought about the night before. Sitting down on the stairs, I put my head in my hands. Metal coldness frosted my forehead as I rubbed my eyes. Moving my arms, I examined the ring. The jade stone sparkled in the sunlight, causing the emblem to appear to come out of its recess, looking almost three-dimensional. As I ran my finger over it, someone stirred from the inside of the cabin. I turned my head just as Nevalin came through the screen door. She was wearing a sky-blue silk nightgown that started at the middle of her cleavage and ended just above the knee. One thin strap ran across her shoulder while the other hung lifelessly on her feminine bicep.

I watched silently as she walked barefoot off the porch, a tube of lotion clutched in her hand. She stepped lightly in the wet grass on her way over to the car where Ontia slumbered. When she reached the car, she bent over into the open back window. Upon bending inside, the bottom of her gown rose so that it gave me a slight glimpse of her blue seated panties. Just before the urge to look away came, Jaynes's voice came from behind me. "Nice view, isn't it?" he said as he patted me on top of my head. He sat down on the porch and joined me in ogling her form. Nevalin must have sensed us staring because she lifted her head slightly and looked at us through her armpit and smiled.

Instantly, I averted my eye to Jaynes, trying play off my slight lapse in judgment. Jaynes – on the other hand – continued to gawk, mouth wide open, allowing his tongue to roll around in the breeze. After twenty minutes, Nevalin withdrew herself from the window and started back toward the cabin. Jaynes stood up, brushing himself off. As Nevalin walked by, he could not take his eyes off her. They followed her from the car to the screen door. He didn't even blink when she walked right past him. His head just turned in time with her footfalls. She walked into the house and let the screen slam close behind him. Jaynes, still stuck in a trance, opened and closed his mouth many times before saying "That girl has got to be mine!"

He turned his head to see that he was talking to me. Almost instantly, his scowl returned to his face. In response, I said, "So what you are going to be mad at me forever now? I didn't mean to leave you by yourself. I got sucked into a rock."

And with that, he fell on the ground laughing. "What is wrong with you?" was barley auditable in between his fits of laughter. "So you expect me to believe you were 'magically' pulled into that boulder. How? There is no such thing as magic," Jaynes said, trying to convince himself it was true.

Before I had a chance to answer, Ontia opened the car door and stepped out. The sun reflected off her flowing black hair as if her skin seemed to disdain the light. She strolled up to me and kissed me on my lips and said "Don't go running off" in the sweetest voice. I then melted like butter back to my sitting position on the porch as Ontia continued on into the cabin. Jaynes started to giggle, putting his hand over a wide smile, trying to contain it. I stood up and walked over to the pile of wood Jaynes must have collected when I was gone. Taking a few scraps of boards, I tossed them onto the pile of embers.

After a few minutes, they started to smoke, eventually catching on fire. Then I walked over to the cooler to take out a few hot dogs to roast. When I returned to the circle of rocks that formed the fire pit, Jaynes was prodding at the wood with a long stick. He slightly moved the ashes underneath to catch the few splinters on top. I took the forked roaster and skewered the hot dogs on the points. Taking a spot out of Jaynes's way, I started to cook the meat over the fire. He walked around the pit, jabbing every now and then at a loose stick or pushing half-torched bark that may have escaped the inferno. As my food darkened in the heat, I watched the flames dance from twig to twig, charring as they went. I thought to myself it seemed as if they were alive – but no, that's not possible. Then one of the flame creatures bowed toward me. As I did a double take, Jaynes walked by, obstructing the fire and blocking my view. When he had passed, all that was in front of me was now just a raging fire.

Then my attention was drawn back to my scorched hot dog – now smoking at the end of my metal rod, which was red from the tip to the handle. Also, the wooden handle was nothing more than white ash in my sizzled hand. You could smell my flesh frying on the uninsulated steel core.

The next set of events took place almost simultaneously. First, Jaynes came back around yelling, "DROP THE DAMN THING, DUMBASS!" Second, Ontia let out a bloodcurdling scream as she and Nevalin came running out of the cabin. Then my reality started again as if someone had pressed PAUSE, allowing me a view of the previous events outside my body. I tossed the metal rod to the ground, causing the hot dog to fall off the spike into the fire. I grasped my injured hand, dusting off the ash. As I looked it over, the ring sucked into my finger, leaving a shiny green stone protruding out of my skin. I flipped my hands over to see my palm, but there was no burn. There was, however, a large dark ruin scarred into my flesh – the same ruin that Grandpa drew on it after graduation. Instantly, I let go of my hand and looked at the other one. The matching ruin also was scarred into the flesh as well, even though it hadn't touched the skewer. My head started to swim as I tried to stand, but my legs became like Jell-O. As my legs gave way, Jaynes dashed over, grabbing me as I fell. After that, all was darkness.

When I came to, Ontia was stroking my head. She and Nevalin were staring at Jaynes, who was mumbling to himself as he paced between his and my bed. On a return trip, he noticed that I was awake. At first he smiled, then it faded into his normal smirk. Then his words became more audible. "So you like to scare people, do yah?"

The girls' eyes turned quickly to view me. I felt Ontia jump slightly in her seat by my side as if surprised. Nevalin reached out to try and touch Jaynes as he stood motionless in the middle of the room. At some point, I went to sit up, but Ontia put her hand softly against my forehead and pushed me back down. The force she used seemed too much for her small frame, but I pawned it off to me being sick and weak.

Jaynes stood in the middle of the room with his arms folded across his chest. "So why didn't you pull the hot dog out of the fire before it burst into flames? The skewer was glowing. I had to dump water on it to cool down before I could touch it." Jaynes spoke while moving his arms in sync with his words. I noticed a black soot mark on one of his palms where he had grabbed the rod. "And why did you pass out afterward? You don't have seizures."

I started to explain to him, but the true story would just make him think I was trying to mess with him. So I made something up. "My mind just blanked out. I must have been out while standing on my feet."

Ontia choked in the background as if holding back a giggle.

Jaynes stood there in his hiking boots glaring at me. It was so quiet, we could hear the woman in the next cabin moaning. Then he let out a loud laugh. After that, the atmosphere changed slowly in our group to a more joyful feeling. Jaynes requested that we move the fun to the fire. Before I left out, he put his hand on my back and said, "Now I think that I'll do your roasting from now on."

I turned around to find a large grin across his face. When he spoke next, the smile stayed. "Now you are careful with that pretty girl. She looks like she could do some damage in the bed. We do not need you passing out again."

I looked at him, awestruck. Then he burst out laughing.

We then proceeded to the fire pit. The girls sat in the folding chairs while Jaynes built up a teepee of wood and set it ablaze. The sun dipped behind the mountains, leaving the valley in darkness. Soon enough, you could hear the frogs croaking down by the lake. The fire slowly consumed the logs, causing light to bask us in its glow. Ontia was lying between her chair and mine. Jaynes and Nevalin were deep in conversation about Paris, France. At one point, bats flew past the camp on their way to the lake. The girls ducked, covering their heads. They squealed "Eew, rats!" as they ran into the cabin, letting the screen door slam behind them.

I looked over at Jaynes, who was sitting in an adjacent chair. His bottle of Labatt Blue was tossed to the side, the beer inside the glass left flowing to the ground where a beetle was scuttling about. He looked at me with a half-cocked grin, and I started to laugh. "The whole thing looked so funny."

Before the words finished coming out, Ontia stuck her head out and said "Guess who gets no snuggle tonight!" then closed the door. With that, Jaynes roared with laughter, nearly falling out of his chair. The girls refused to come out for the rest of the night, so my brother and I sat the rest of the night by the fire. At one point, I went to say something to him. But when I glanced over, he was snoring in his chair, holding yet another half-finished bottle of beer.

CHAPTER 5

Claws of the Enemy

I SAT through the twilight hours in my canvas chair; a small bundle of sticks that I managed to gather through the night sat by my side. Slowly I tossed random twigs into the fire, which was pleading with me to keep it alive. Once they were used up, I leaned back to watch the fire. The flames greedily consumed the round scraps of wood. It flickered for a moment, and finally, it fell back down into the coals that glowed below. The embers also faded after a while, so I stood up and folded the chair. Sliding it into its accompanying bag, I walked over to the cabin. Before I could reach it, a sound of someone clearing their throat broke through the silence across the valley. I spun around to try and find the source of the disruption. The light of the moon beamed onto the campsite, illuminating the car. There on the ground underneath the door was Lamel. His arms were draped around his knees.

He sat there rocking back and forth, mumbling inaudibly. As I drew closer, I notice a multitude of long deep gashes running the length of his arm, making them resemble some sort of bloody ladder. The fronts of his legs were similarly marred. Deep red blood flowed down to the ground, pooling around the soles of his shoes. His head was tucked into the cup that his legs and torso made. When I was close enough to touch him, his face appeared from the fold. He reminded me of a child who just threw a tantrum and the snot was oozing out of his nostrils.

He sniffed slightly to clear away the mucus that had drained out of his nose. Whatever remained of the goo, he wiped away with a slow pass of his arm. He looked up into my face as if he had been waiting in the same spot for years. His big almond eyes flooded with water daring to overflow. His lower lip quivered like a scared rabbit as I spoke first. "How did this happen to you?"

He continued to rock for a while before stammering out, "The vamps. It was the vamps. They stormed into my house almost an hour after you left, searching for the Book of Sight." He broke off midsentence, then shivered violently and continued, "I was just barely able to sneak out of the back. Before they noticed I had fled, I could hear their howls as they gave chase in the forest."

"But why come here? I can't help you." I was speaking fast as I maintained a look of concern.

He opened his wide eyes and a quizzical look came across his face, but when he spoke this time, his tone was that of shock, "What do you mean you can't do anything? Of course you can. You're the Keeper of the realms now. You are the only one now who can keep the balance. That's why I gave you the ring. It was your inheritance."

"But what am I supposed to do with some gaudy bobble? Try to shine sunlight in their eyes? I mean come now, I'm a human. I'm sorry, Lamel, but I'm not the person who you thought I am."

The words flowed out of my mouth as a wave of verbs that crashed against Lamel's face. The look on his face shifted many times, then he settled on one of disapproval. His next thoughts seem to project onto his face before he could speak them.

"Your grandfather was the greatest of all, so I know he taught you some useful spells to fight with," he said with a smile. The air started to grow thick around the clearing in preparation of the dawn.

"Spells – I don't know what you are talking about. My grandfather only knew cheap parlor tricks. He taught me how to palm small objects and different quick-hand tricks, but nothing that I could say was real magic."

Lamel winced in pain as he giggled to himself. Then he said, "Lexxy, you got to be joking with me. You're a child of the Gate, and you don't know the most common of spells?" A smirk came to his lips.

"I TOLD YOU NOT TO CALL ME THAT!" I screamed unintentionally.

"Don't call you what – Lexxy or child of the Gate? But that is who you are," Lamel answered back, unaffected by my elevated tone.

"No. What? Wait a minute, don't call me Lexxy! That 'children in the Gate' thing – I have no clue what you are talking about." I said, "Aaahh, that doesn't matter. Hey, by any chance, can I use some of your manna? I used mine all up running, and I'm really in a lot of pain even though it might not look it," Lamel spoke in an airy kind of voice, almost as if he were telling a joke that only he got.

"Let you use my manna? What do you think this is – Dungeons and Dragons or something? I don't have any manna. And this is the real world. We can't really use magic," I spoke as if trying to still convince myself that I had to be dreaming.

"Ah, so you still won't believe unless it's staring you in the face. OK, I see I'm going to have to show what is real in your world." Lamel reached over and clutched my ankle. "The transfer may leave you a little lightheaded, but you should be able to deal with it."

As his words ended, he began to sing some sort of song – low enough to be heard by me as a soft hum only. His lips blurred for a second. Then I felt inside my body a slow stream of energy slide out of my leg and calf muscles. My knees quivered slightly; It was like opening your eyes in a swimming pool. Just before my legs were about to give way, Lamel let go. Instantly, I felt a new rush of energy like I just ate four chocolate energy bars. It flooded my legs like water filling a glass, from the soles of my feet up. Soon afterward, my vision returned to normal. Lamel, on the other hand, was a totally different story. After releasing my leg, he took his hand and closed it, leaving only his index finger extended. Then he drew tight circles around all the cuts, and after a few passes around each one, the skin just reached for each other, leaving light scars where the gashes were and if his one hand could not reach a cut. He would touch one finger to another, causing an electrical arc between them, the light flashing in the predawn hours.

An hour had passed when I heard breathing just behind me. Turning around, I saw Jaynes standing there with a smug look on his face and his arms crossed. Clearly, he had been there awhile watching us talk. "So, li (hic) ttle baby Gates found himself a new friend," he said in a drunken stammer. He rocked back and forth on his heels for a while then said with a drunken slur, "You boys don't get yourselves in any trouble now. And, Lexxy, don't give him all your power. It's special!" He turned around and stumbled to the cabin afterward. Lamel seemed undisturbed by him, but his calmness sent a small shiver up my back.

Pawning off his comment to his drunken stupor, I gave my attention back to Lamel, as he was attempting to stand upright. So I reached down to lend him a hand, which he took in turn. His limbs quivered under his mass. I grasped under his left arm and hoisted him onto my shoulder. We look like a four legged contestant in a race as we hobbled back to my camping chair. He collapsed down on the canvas fabric and the aluminum frame.

"So what is next?" I asked into the night.

Lamel looked up and said, "Well, as soon as I regain my strength, I'll be on my way. The quest you have been set upon is dangerous enough without me adding to your problems. But I could use a drink of water, if you have it to spare I mean."

His response struck me as odd. "The only quest I could possibly be on has to be me trying to relax," I said as I was getting a bottle of water out of the cooler. When I returned with the bottle, he was standing on his feet – shifting his weight left and right, squishing out the dirt from underneath the soles of his shoes.

"Well, Mr. Gates, I'll leave you to your relaxation. I am going to find my mother. She said she was going to the Jade Citadel. I think I will try there first," he said accepting the bottle.

After he finished off all the water in a gulp, Lamel bowed to me then turned and took off so fast into the night. That dust kicked up into a thick smokescreen to cover his exit.

I stood there in early morning, possibly minutes before the sun started its daily track into the sky, the dust still aloft in the wind. That was when I heard it for the first time – a sound that would make your skin flee from your bone. It started in a loud growl, pitching to a high squeal, and ended in a deep long growl. The leaves would vibrate on their stems as the echo flew past. Now hearing this, I turned to run into the wooden building in desperation for safety; for whatever made that noise, I wanted no part of that! Even though the distance was only twenty feet away, it seemed to take forever to make it to the door, so I turned around while opening it to chance a last peek. In the fading darkness, something came out of the woods. It had an elongated body like a lizard, but its nose and snout were as a wolf. Its full body was covered with light hair that you could barely make out in the morning light.

The animal sniffed around till it eventually found the car. It walked over and started to sniff the ground near the front end, then climbed on top silently as a cat through grass. Standing on its thick hind legs, it howled its horrible call. The creature's tale hung off the back, steering it. Then its head swiveled left and right. That's when I think it caught a glance of me. Because it got off the roof in a single bound and ran lumbering back into the forest, its tail slashing a tree near the parameter as it passed.

When it was fully gone from my sight, I pulled my head into the cabin, as the rest of my body was already concealed within. When I finally turned around, everyone was staring at me from the bunks. Nevalin was on Ontia's bed; they were entangled with each other. Their eyes reflected the fear they felt. Jaynes was lying on his mattress, facing the girls, blanket still cast about his body as if he jumped when he heard the howl. "Dude what was that?" he said when my mind was focused on him.

"I don't know, but it looked as scary as it sounded," I replied. I walked over to the girls and wrapped my arms around them and said, "It's OK, baby, I won't let anything happen to you or your friend".

Ontia looked at me and started to speak, but was cut off by Nevalin, "I don't want to stay here another night if something like that is skulking around. Just the call alone was enough to know that I don't want to see it up close."

CHAPTER 6

The Trip Home

WE spent the early morning huddled in the cabin – Ontia and I in our bed, while Nevalin curled up with Jaynes. She really didn't want to be alone and on her own. As the early morning turned to noon, I left the shanty and went to investigate the area where I had seen the creature. All around the car, there were claw marks, as if the thing just walked on its nails. Next, I went to the tree that it had whipped with its tail. There was a large fresh scar in the wood, deep enough so you could see the white wood. The rings that marked the tree's age stood out like veins in a pale man's hand. The outside edges of the void looked as if someone had chopped at it with an ax, as there were razorlike cuts that made grooves inside the gouge that ran to the center.

A chill ran through my spine at the thought of getting hit with such a weapon. From the look of this cut, it could free flesh from bone with ease. I stood staring at the mark, and then I heard a noise about twenty yards from where I stood. My eyes raked the ground and combed the trees for the source. When I failed in that attempt, I turned around to join our group in repacking the car. Ontia came out of the cabin holding a small bag. She set it on the wooden table and started to pull makeup out. Each bottle that was pulled out was set on the table in an organized order. Light colors of nail polish, then dark colors. Bottles of hair spray and suntan lotion were placed behind them because they were larger. A nail file and a pair of clippers were set inside the semicircle she had constructed.

Nevalin voice came from just behind the screen door. "Damn, Oni! You have all day to put on makeup. Get up and help us get ready to leave."

Ontia looked at the door as if she could see right through it and said, "I want to get this done before we leave, because I won't have time to do it in the car."

Nevalin responded with a quick toot of air through her nose. Then Ontia returned to doing her nails, as though she had never been interrupted on the first place. I stood at the car attempting to put everything back in, which was not very difficult being as we had less to take home than we originally brought with us. Jaynes and Nevalin walked back and forth, depositing our stuff in a pile at the back of the vehicle. I took it and put it all in the trunk.

The sun was already starting its trip down the sky to the earth when we finally finished. We all jumped in and drove down to return our key to the main building. Afterward, we drove down to the lake; the water was so smooth and calm. Not a breeze disturbed its complacent movement. Nevalin and Jaynes stripped down to their swimsuits and dove into the shallow waters. They playfully splashed each other in the cool liquid. Jaynes would submerge and come out under an unwitting Nevalin and toss her into the air. She would let out a great squeal then fall backward off his shoulders.

Ontia had gotten a lawn chair out and was gesturing for me. When I was close, she said, "Would you rub lotion on me, baby?"

I grabbed the sunscreen lotion out of her purse in the front seat of the car, squirted out a nice portion, and started to rub her back with it. A few times, she let out a moan, but by the time I had finished lathering her up, she had fallen asleep. I could hear her soft breath escaping her mouth. Leaving her, I tossed the lotion on top of her bag and then went to watch Jaynes and Nevalin play. Ontia woke just in time to watch the sunset wrapped in my arms. Nevalin said something to Jaynes about how romantic the mood was, but her comment was lost to the wind. The only person that mattered at that moment had her head resting on my chest.

After the sun hid behind the horizon, Ontia and Nevalin pulled out their bottle of wine. The girls insisted that they had to have a few glasses. Then we all piled back into the car to start our trip home. Jaynes took a park road that led back to the highway. Nevalin sat quietly in the passenger seat, staring out at the fields flying by. Ontia rested her head on my lap, and I tried to watch the oncoming traffic. For the most part, Jaynes is a good driver, but he tends to speed a lot. It took at least one and a half hours for us to reach the city limits. I struggled to fight the slumber of boredom, while Jaynes seemed unaffected as he drove on.

Just before we could see the city tollbooths, a bird flew into our windshield. Jaynes slammed on the brakes, causing the car to screech to a halt. It's a good thing there weren't many cars on the road, or our sudden stop would have caused a major accident. Jaynes then pulled over, got out of the car, and called my name. When I was out, I saw him just staring at the windshield. I looked to see what was so interesting, and there sitting on the hood of our car was what only could be described as a sprite. She was wearing blue feathers as a cloak and had a beak of the fowl atop her head. The little woman was staring at Jaynes with black eyes that made up have her face. She had transparent wings sticking out the back of her wardrobe. She was no bigger than twelve inches, small enough to fit in the palm of your hand, no problem.

Jaynes looked over to me and said, "This bird won't move, and it keeps staring at me."

I looked down at the sprite as she shifted her gaze to me. When she spoke, her voice was as a bird's call, "Are you the one who will bring the realms together?"

All I could do was just stand there with my mouth wide open. The rest of what she said was lost to the noise of the traffic passing us by. All I could do was just nod my head.

Jaynes – on the other side of the car – had to call out, "Dude, Why are you nodding to a bird? Have you lost your mind or something?" When he said this, the little woman's face went from delighted to a scowl. She put her hands on her hips and tapped her foot, glaring at him. She glanced at me and said, "That guy is really stupid, isn't he? If you are responding to the things I say, I must not be an ordinary bird then, right?"

I could not help but giggle. If Jaynes would have heard her say that, all hell would have broken loose.

Jaynes continued to press the issue of the bird on his car. "What if it takes a shit or something? Then I would have to clean it off."

After a while of me ignoring him and staring at the bird, he swung his arms at it. The fairy looked at him and then took flight. Her wings beat the air, generating a humming noise. Then she started to hover for a second, looking at me. Her final words were "I'll meet you at Gatesholm where we can have a conversation, without those of lesser intelligence bothering us."

With that, she took to the air and soared off into the blue sky.

CHAPTER 7

The Deal

AFTER he accepted that I was not talking to the bird, we got back into the car and continued on our way home. We stopped at the interstate tollbooths, Nevalin waved to one of the tellers. The man in the booth's mouth dropped, and he started to wave his hand vigorously. She giggled to herself as if she told a good joke. We passed the Walden gallery mall, with its parking lot a-bustle with customers. Nevalin choose to live in a large hotel close to the airport, and Ontia was staying with her.

After dropping off the girls, we stopped at a small diner to grab a bite to eat. It was more of a in-and-out type of thing. Enjoying our meal in the car, Jaynes drove the short distance to where my newly inherited home was positioned. As we pulled close to where the driveway should be, there was this massive clump of trees with a dirt path one and a half cars wide. He pulled in and followed the trail like it was supposed to be there. So I said nothing, thinking this must be the effect of the ring. So he parked, got out the car, and proceeded up to a swirling mass of energy.

On my hand, the ring hummed with a pearlescent glow. When I slipped it off, the shine dimmed to its original luster. Looking around, all the trees faded to nothing, leaving the stately manor in place of the vortex. Jaynes was already ascending the stairs, keys jingling in hand. He stopped and turned at the threshold. "Hey, what are you doing? Are you coming?" His words snapped me out of my awestruck stupor. Clutching the ring in my hand, I walked forward to join him.

As we proceeded through the door, I noticed there was a group of mice huddled around a small crumb of cheese. When we entered the room, the ketch of rodents ripped the cheese apart and scampered off. Three of them raced to a nearby chair, three to the television stand. Two dashed to the china cabinet, and one climbed to the top of the fireplace. He sat there, chewing his booty.

A thought flicked through my head. Quickly I shoved the ring onto my finger. The room flashed with a bright light, causing my eyes to blink. When I opened my eyes, the mouse on the mantel had transformed into a man no taller than my middle finger, wearing the hide of a mouse with its head set atop his own. If he were crawling, he would look like a mouse. The man looked up from his meal and waved his hand. As a reflex, I returned the gesture with a flick of my own.

Jaynes, who was just in front of me, didn't notice. He walked over, turning on the TV, and plopped down on the sofa. The screen came alive, playing some cartoon. "Oh, I love *The Sword in the Stone*," he commented.

A grin spread across the little man's face. He crossed his legs and tossed another crumb into his mouth. His beady eyes focused on the movie. Keeping watch on our guest, I moved and sat in the plush chair. The three of us sat in silence until the end of the cartoon. Jaynes stretched and yawned, rubbing his head. Then he said, "It's getting late, I think I'll be heading home." He stood up, glancing at the fireplace. While reaching for his keys, in one fluid motion, he grabbed a magazine and hurled it through the air.

The periodical flew through the air and smacked the fireplace just under the mouse man. Startled, the man dashed behind Grandpa's wedding photo. Jaynes rushed over to snatch up the frame, revealing a small hole in the chimney.

"You need to call an exterminator. This house has always been infested with those things." Defeated, he set it down. "Do you know how long it had been there?"

"No," I replied dismissively.

He walked over, scooping up his keys in his left hand. He extended his right to me. After accepting his farewell, Jaynes stepped out the door and closed it.

Once I was alone, I proceeded to the kitchen. I stopped to get a glass of milk. On the door was an unopened pack of cheese. I took out one slice and broke it into fours. Stepping back in the living room, I placed the pile on the mantel, sat back down on the sofa, and waited. After more than an hour, I started to drift into a light sleep.

Dreams of a long-bearded man wearing robes with fields of blue covered in stars, and pulling swords from anvils washed in my head. It was the sound of lips smacking that woke me from my slumber. Ears twitched with every close of his mouth. Looking properly, there was the same little man sitting legs dangling over the edge of the wood. Then he spoke with a squeaky Australian voice. "Thanks, me lad. It's been a while since I had me a bit of fresh cheese. Old Zavies and I had an arrangement: he leaves out fresh food for us, and we keep things clean. It has been a while since our deal has been honored. So who is the Keeper now, boy?"

I replied, "What's a Keeper? For that matter, who are you?"

With a grin, he stood up and flipped the mouse head off his head. Doing a bow, he said, "Oh, forgive me. My Name is Jangle – Thomas B. Jangle. I'm the mayor of the community of brownies underneath us. I remember you from when you where just a wee sprout. We even had a run-in when you rescued me from your brother. Do you remember you weren't any more than ten? That boy always was a little too much darkness for my taste." He finished speaking and shoved another hunk of cheese in his mouth, smacking away.

Thinking back, there was a time when Jaynes had a mouse trapped under a jar. He told me to watch it and ran off to get something to keep it in. Grandpa called me downstairs, and when I stood up, I knocked the jar over. "So, Lexxy my boy, who is the new Keeper?" Thomas's voice started growing irate.

"My grandfather passed away, and he left the house in his will. The lawyer said it was notarized. So I guess that makes me the new Keeper," I said.

When Thomas started to talk next, it was more to him than to me. "What? Just like Zavies to go off on some dangerous adventure and not tell me. Well, I suppose if the council has approved you, then all is well. They did approve, right?"

Confused, I replied, "Council? The common council has nothing to do with the distribution of inheritance."

"You know nothing, boy! The Council of Antiquate. It's the only council that really matters when it comes to magic. The magic worlds exist in parallel with the mortal realm. The rulings that the council put out take precedence over any law humans deem important. The arrogance of some people – to think that they can control the world!"

He stopped talking. We sat in silence for a while until the sound of movement came from the hole behind the picture. The sound stopped, and a woman just a half a head shorter than Thomas stepped from behind with her hands on her hips.

She wore black shoes, a green pleated skirt with a red shirt tucked in, and a green bow sat in her auburn hair. She shot Thomas a dirty look then began to speak. "You're out gallivanting again, with everybody starving down there." She turned her head and almost passed out at the sight of me. "Oh, here is the holdup. Excuse me, is my husband bothering you?"

"Not at all" I replied.

"Good, he does have a tendency to talk out of control," the lady said.

Thomas started to grumble then said audibly, "Lexxy, let me introduce this ball of spitfire. This is Geraldine Jingles, my wife."

Geraldine turned and did a little curtsey. "I know you men are all wrapped in a good discussion, but did you ask him?"

Thomas shook his head. "Woman, You can't just jump into things like that. You have to exchange pleasantries first," he replied.

Ensnared by the question, I spoke, "What is it that you want to ask me?"

Her face relaxed into a pleasant smile that gleamed through her teeth. "Well, we had an arrangement with your grandfather. We would keep the house clean and safe if he would bring us fresh food. It's a trifle to search for one's food while on guard duty. This deal was brokered when we first settled in many years ago. We ask that you do the same, for it is beneficial to all involved."

Her argument was sound. "I don't see any reason I should change anything if everybody is happy. Yes I will bring you fresh food, how much would you like?"

Thomas responded to my question, "A human basket of food will last us a year. That will suffice."

Clapping his hands together, Thomas said, "Now that is taken care of. Alexander, what don't you know of our realm?"

Shaking her head, Geraldine turned and started to walk through the hole. "You boys have fun, and Thomas, don't come back too late for dinner." Then she disappeared inside. "I have another deal for you. How about tomorrow I show you what your grandfather left for you in our position."

"That sounds like a plan. You have a good night, Thomas."

"Yes, yes you too, lad." Thomas smiled, stretched his back, and he too was gone into the darkness. I went upstairs to my room with sleep still in my eyes. The Land of Nod beckoned me to my bed.

CHAPTER 8

Unexpected Guests

IT wasn't the morning sun beaming through the window that woke me. Nor was it the buzzing of the alarm clock blinking 8:45 a.m. No, it was the unseen body pouncing on my chest that jarred me from my slumber. Arms flailing, I groped for the bed stand. Finding my target, I slipped the ring onto my finger. Morning light flashed in my eyes when I opened them. A boy not taller than my pinky was tramping my blankets squeaking, "Father told me to wake you up, Father told me to wake you up." Every word was accompanied by another pounce.

"I'm awake, stop jumping on me."

The tiny boy turned on one foot and darted down to the floor. There was a sound of heels on wood as he exited. Getting out of bed, the frigid planks frosted my feet. I walked to the window and drew the blinds open. There, pulling up the driveway, was a black sedan. Leaving the window, I got dressed and trotted down the stairs.

Before I made it through the kitchen, there was a knock at the front door. Standing there was a man in a black suit with a wide brim hat. His short thin face had pale skin, his eyes a cold green. He wore an unnatural pearly white grin as the door swung open. Another man stood behind him, his white-gloved hand holding an umbrella, also dressed in a black suit. He was taller than the first, but his skin was just as pale. The man in the lead spoke first with a smooth voice. "We are representatives of the council of antiquities, May we come in?"

I paused for a minute. Then Thomas jumped from a hole just above the doorframe screaming "NO! NO! NO!" He landed on my shoulder, brandishing a sword the size of one you would see in a cocktail drink. "NO, YOU CANNOT! You must not grant that foul creature entrance here."

The smaller man's smile grew wider, baring his long silver canine teeth. Then it changed into a long smirk. "Still alive, Jingles? Would have thought a cat had digested you by now."

"Better watch that sun, Lucius. Never know when you'll burst into flames," Thomas spat back.

The taller man touched Lucius on the shoulder then spoke in a low, deep voice, "I beg your forgiveness, Prince, but – "

"Yes, yes, Octavian, I'm fully aware why we are here. I am playing courier for my father." Lucius reached into his pocket, pulled out an envelope, and held it out.

I grasped the package, trying to take it away, but Lucius still kept a hold on it. His eyes bore into mine. I glanced passed him at Octavian. When my eyes came back to Lucius, he released the letter as if it were something revolting. The look on his face was of disgust and shock. The duet then turned on their heels and walked back to the car. Octavian tailing keeping the umbrella opened till Lucius was in the car.

Thomas sheathed his sword and said, "Damn vampires, they think they can control everything. You, my boy, are full of surprises. You didn't feel anything, did you?"

"No?" I replied in a questioning tone.

"You felt nothing at all? You didn't feel woozy, maybe not in full control of your faculties?"

"No. I was just asking myself: why is he glaring at me? Then I looked at the other guy, and he was staring me down as well," I said, closing the door.

I opened the envelope as I walked over to the sofa chair and sat down. Thomas ran down my arm with the agility of a cat. Once on the arm of the seat, he hopped the short distance to the in-table.

Thomas paced back and forth for a while, and then he stopped and cupped his hands around his mouth and yelled "Geraldine!"

A minute later, she stepped from behind the picture, hands on her hips. "What is it now, Thomas?"

Thomas turned to look at her and said, "Would you please bring Alex his grandfather's field guide?"

Geraldine shifted her weight to her other foot and said, "Now, Thomas, you know that cannot leave the study. That was the problem Zavies had in the first place."

Baffled, I said, "Why can't it leave the study? It's only a book, right?"

Geraldine spoke to me this time. "You aren't too keen on surprises, are you? Just go to the study. I will meet you up there. Thomas, you need to come feed the children."

Thomas shrugged, then turned to me and said, "Would you be as kind as to place me on the mantel near my wife?"

I got to my feet and placed the envelope down without looking inside. Thomas sat in the palm of my hand. I crossed the distance between in a few strides. He hopped off my arm once it was extended, and with a flash of his cloak's tale, he and Geraldine disappeared behind the frame.

Through the kitchen, up the first set of stairs, down the hall of bedrooms, and up the second flight of steps to the sturdy door that lead to the study. I reached out for the glass knob, but before I could release it, the gaps between the door and the frame started to glow with a blinding green light. Releasing the knob, I jumped back. The glow subsided, and the door swung in, allowing access.

The room I entered was not the same room as before. Instead of a small study, there was a long gallery of bookshelves that extended from a center aisle to the walls. Each row of shelves had a letter from *A* to *M* on my left, and *N* to *Z* on my right. Below each letter, there were wooden tables. Lamps were set atop them for light. From the slick tiled marble floor to its cathedral ceiling, books towered above me. Natural light filtered in from the six large skylights in the roof. I had never been in a grander library in my life; it was as if I stepped out of my home and into a large castle. The center aisle ran from the door I had entered through to a large portrait of a man reading under a large willow tree surrounded by small children.

The faces of the shelves had a large sheet of frosted sheet glass on their fronts that could be slid open, allowing access to the books contained therein. Looking down the center, I saw Geraldine standing on the table between *F* and *G*. She had changed since she was downstairs. Now she wore a white sundress with red shoes and a red bow in her hair. When I approached her, she pointed down aisle *G* and said, "There is a door down at the end of this row marked with a *G*. Walk through it, but as you near it, keep in mind the object you're searching for."

She smirked and then continued, "Be truly careful going through these doors. Sometimes there is a steep price to be paid to gain entry. Unfortunately, your grandfather found that out the hard way."

I thanked her for the tip and started to walk down the row. The whole time I thought, *Why couldn't a book be taken out of here? Was it a really big book? Did the book need this much security because it was valuable? What could Grandpa have written in it that needed to be kept safe?*

CHAPTER 9

Dimension Dragon

THREE paces away from it, the door slowly creaked open. Immediately my nose was bombarded with the smell of blood-soaked earth. I stretched my arms out to feel a way through. Wooden planks paneled along the walls. My steps echoed in the staggering darkness. After a few steps forward on the stone surface, the door slammed shut, sealing me in.

As I continued walking in the dark atmosphere, florescent green rocks started to come to life against the ceiling. The glowing rocks ran in a line down the center of this cave. I traveled a long ways down the path. At the end of the corridor, I came to a flap of leather with a divide down the center, creating a kind of doorway.

Shouldering my way through them, I came to a huge cavern. I looked around, noticing there were also glowing rocks in the walls here – although these were smothered by the same leathery flap that I just pushed through. The light barely filtered to the floor, making it difficult to move. More than a few times, I stumbled over bones and carcasses.

I had made it a considerable way in when a deep baritone voice boomed loudly off the cave walls, "Welcome, young Gates. I have been expecting you for some time."

The voice, although calm, was disorientating. In this dark room, someone had been waiting for me. The thought to dash back the way I came flicked through my head. He had been expecting me; I started to worry.

Then the voice spoke again. "It's true. You do resemble your mother."

With that, I stopped, frozen in place.

Then the voice came once more, "Don't be alarmed. I guess I have you at a disadvantage. I see your grandfather has raised you well. Your instincts are keen. Good, you're going to need them."

Far in the distance, barely visible, someone stood to their feet. The figure raised his hands into the air then lowered them down to his sides swiftly. The walls shuttered. Then there came a sound of leather sliding over rock. I looked around, and slowly, the leather that was blocking the entrance slid around the sides of the cave. As it did, the glow stones regained their original shine.

With the light of the stones illuminating the room, it was apparent that the leathery substance was wings, and they were being retracted into the man's back. He was at least six feet tall. His face was unnaturally reptilian. His almond eyes had slits in them, like a snake's. His nose was wide at the base. His lips were thin, his smile sharp and pointed.

The last of the wings slid beneath his cape. He started to walk toward me with smooth strides. I stepped back, scared of his approach.

"Don't be so apprehensive, I am not going to hurt you. Let me introduce myself. My name is Crono Dregus – the Dimension Dragon. I know who you are Alexander Gates, grandchild of Zavies and Gertrude Gates. Zavies was my good friend during his long life. I made him a promise to train his children to defend the family land known as Gatesholm. I, Dregus, will teach you what your human life did not. First, have you made your claim to this land?"

Shock was the only feeling I could describe. "Claim to this land? Gate helm – what's that?" I questioned.

Dregus shook his head and rolled his eyes. "Well, I guess we will have to start from the beginning. We won't have time for me to explain everything now, but you will get a crash course. Am I right in assuming you have heard from the Council of Antiquities?"

"How could you have known that?" I asked.

Dregus looked around and said, "How about we change our surroundings a little?" Then he snapped his fingers twice, and the cave shook. A few stalactites fell from the ceiling as the walls shifted into themselves. In an instant, we were in a study with chairs and a desk off against a wall. Books in piles lined the other three. It was not a grand study, but it looked ancient.

Dregus gestured for me to sit. He sat in a seat adjacent to me. Taking a deep breath, he spoke, "Do you know why our good friend Thomas was so adamant about not letting Lucius in?" He paused then said, "It is because he is a vampire. In fact, he is the eldest son of the current Dracula."

"Wait a minute, you want me to believe that Count Dracula is real?" I replied, unbelieving.

Dregus looked at me and said, "You can believe that there are brownies running behind the walls of your home, but to believe in vampires is a stretch for your mind? Come now, young Gates, just hear me out.

"In this dimension called 'If,' vampire, werewolf, and sapiens have always kept each other's population in check. Vampires drink the blood of sapiens, werewolves kill vampires, and sapiens hunt both. Vampires – as most legends say – can fly, change form, and even mesmerize the weak-minded. The sun, cutting off one's head, or a stake through the heart will usually kill a vampire. Werewolves, on the other hand, are the most well known of shifters. They can be killed by severing their heads also, but silver works on both.

"Long before the time Sapiens call BC, vampires lived in nesting clans. When in these groupings, they were savage and vicious. Fighting for placement or food would be their way of ruling. The different clans battled for feeding rights on most populations of Sapiens. The older a vampire is, the stronger it becomes. In this, the oldest vampire in the clan became leader. After 20 AD, vampires organized their smaller clans into a large group. They called themselves the Vampire Nation. The strongest clan leaders fought for leadership of the nation every few centuries.

"In the fifteenth century, a prince named Vlad Tepis – or Vlad Dracule of Wallachia – fought a gruesome war with the Turkish army. His favorite punishment was to carve a tree trunk into a pike. Then he would impale the prisoner on the spike rectum first and let the weight slowly pull them down. He had even been sighted eating dinner among the forest of bodies from time to time. This led Sapiens to claim that he was a vampire. Since his name struck fear into the hearts of Sapiens, the Vampire Nation decreed from then on the leader would be known as Count Dracula. Any female leaders of the nation were known as Countess.

"The current Count Dracula is Darius Dracman. You have met his son, Lucius. There are tales that he has a female child, but little is known of her. You must be careful when dealing with vampires. A sapiens's greatest weapon is the fact that vampires can't enter their dwelling unless otherwise invited in. This is why Thomas did not want you to let him in. If you had, then he could have entered anytime he wanted, whether you wanted him here or not."

Dregus stopped and looked up at the ceiling then shook his head.

"This will have to be the end of our lesson. There are so many things to teach you, yet so little time for you to learn. Would you come close to me? I have a gift to impart that will allow me to communicate with you, no matter the distance. Within this gift, I will continue your instruction."

I stood out of my seat and walked over to him. When I was close, I reached out my hand, palm up.

He chuckled and said, "Lean closer."

When I did so, he reached out his hand, placing it just inches in front of my forehead. He then mumbled a few incoherent words, and an arc of electricity jumped from his palm to my head. With a flash of white light, I was instantly back in the library, sitting in a chair at the end of a row.

CHAPTER 10

Thomas's Army

ON the table to my left – snoring, a leg crossed propped up on the lamp – was Geraldine. I stood to my feet and began to walk to the door leading to the rest of the house. Just as I did, she awoke, smiled, and said, "I hope you learn your lessons well. It is an honor to be instructed by a dragon. Oh, by the way, Thomas wants to speak to you down in the kitchen. I will see you later."

She stood up from the lamp, turned, and placed one hand on the brass surface. The lamp slid aside, providing access to a staircase. I watched as Geraldine descended into its depths. When she was gone, the light slid back into place.

I walked down to the kitchen, only pausing to use the bathroom. When I opened the door, the whole floor was covered in brownies. They were all different heights and weights. Their outfits held an assortment of decorations they bore. Some brownies had feathers for capes, others with soda can openers for necklaces and nutshells for hats. The colors of the general garments were either brown or red.

They were all grouped in squares of alternating colors. Thomas addressed me as I stepped in. "Hey, Alexander, come over here."

He was standing on the stove in between the burners. As I started to walk, the blocks of brownies parted. I only took three steps, but I displaced at least four or five different groups. They scurried with precision in my wake to get back into position, never leaving their block formation.

"This is our Brownie Armed Forces. What do you think?" Thomas said with his chest puffed out.

Looking down, there were at least forty groups spread out over the floor of the kitchen.

"Our regiments are set up for inspection. Zavies established this for the protection of Gatesholm. We are your eyes and ears. Nothing happens here that we don't know. Do you have any military experience, my boy?"

"No, sorry. Grandpa asked me if I wanted to follow after him and go into the navy. I instead went to college. The military never was really my thing. When I told him no, he looked a little disappointed, but he'd never admit it to me."

"Yeah, that was Zavies's way. If things didn't go his way, he never lost a stride. He would just keep moving," Thomas responded. Then he turned to his troops and said, "All right, this is Alexander. Some of you may know him, some may not. That does not matter. We are here to make certain that the Vortex remains in the hands of the light. Alexander is now our Keeper. Zavies left orders to follow the Keeper till the gate falls."

There was a slight mumbling in the crowd.

"I, in turn, told him that it will never fall – not as long as we brownies draw breath!"

The audience roared with cheer.

"Alexander, would you like to say a few words to our troops?" Thomas gestured to me.

I cleared my throat and said, "I am not my grandfather, but he did raise me to do the best I can. That is what I intend on doing. No matter what, I will do what is right. Thank you."

The crowd roared again with cheer.

Buttons spoke up once more. "Now I want to thank you for your attendance. Spread the word of Keeper's arrival to all. Dismissed!"

The army broke rank and became a mass of little people. Watching the brownies exit was like staring at an ant nest busy at work. They filed out into unseen exits scattered throughout the kitchen – some underneath tiles, others hidden behind electrical outlets or tucked behind the refrigerator. Thomas watched from his perch on the stove, shining his sword with a small handkerchief. He wore a look of pride as he watched his kin file away.

Once we were left alone standing in the kitchen, Thomas turned to me again saying, "So what did old Dregus have to say? Come on, boy, don't leave me in the dark."

I took a moment and started to speak. "He told me about vampires . . ." I tried to think back to the ancient study, but there was something in the way. I tried to continue to speak, but no sound left my vocal box.

Then Dregus's voice spoke in my mind. "Although Thomas is our friend, it does not mean he needs to know the details of our relationship."

Instantly I thought, "Is he blocking my speech?"

As the words formed in my head, Dregus answered, "Yes. I am stopping you form saying something foolish. This is what you should tell him."

As the words came from him, they fell from my lips. "He told me about the vampires that came here. He explained their powers and cautioned against dealing with them."

"That Lucius is as rotten as his father. Can't trust a vampire, the whole lot of them will suck you dry," Thomas said, seeming happy with the information. He slid his sword back into its sheath and walked over to one of the burners on the stove. "Well, I think I'll turn in for the night. Sleep well, boy. Maybe tomorrow I'll take you on a tour of the forest outside." Then with a snap of his fingers, he disappeared in a puff of smoke.

I glanced at my watch – 10:30 p.m. showed green in the dimness of the kitchen. Stretching my arms and yawning, I walked to the living room to sit in the armchair. "Wow, how long was I with Dregus?" I thought.

Dregus spoke once again in my head. "Well, young one, time moves differently in my cave – one of the precautions your grandfather took in its design. It is so no one can stay long enough in an attempt to remove me. Had your intentions been nefarious, time would have risen to the speed light travels, ageing you out of existence."

I thought more to myself than to him. "Are you always going to jump into my thoughts?"

"No, only if there is something I could add," Dregus's voice sounded in my head.

"So everything I think you can hear? What about pictures, can you see through my eyes?"

Dregus chuckled then said, "Boy, I'm not interested in your trivial thoughts. Those are yours. Once you have learned all that I have to teach, then I will withdraw from your mind. As a dimension dragon, I have a responsibility to oversee all realms. In some, I am not needed, but in others – that is quite a different story."

"What is your job here, Dregus?" I said.

Dregus let out a sigh and then said, "I hold this dimension together. My cave is the focal point of your dimension, or the Nexus. When your grandfather discovered me here, he built this house to protect it. There is darkness in your realm that wishes to control the Nexus."

Dregus fell silent for a moment, so I spoke up, "I don't understand why this darkness would want to control your cave?"

There was a pause. I could hear crickets chirping outside waiting for his answer. Then Dregus said, "The Nexus is the point in which all magic flows through into your world. You, as Keeper, have the ability to control it. When you are in full control of this energy, the only limit to what you can do is your imagination. Currently, you have no idea how to use any of it. However, that will change once you have adapted to your role."

I reached over and picked up the envelope and pulled out the document. It had a watermark behind the writing of a large tree in a circle. Dated the same day as the reading of my grandfather's will, it said:

Dear Mr. Gates,

You are required to come to the council room in Subterra in order to be granted full ownership of Gatesholm. The location of Subterra is a magical secret and therefore cannot be told to anyone. You have to locate it on your own. You have two days upon acceptance of this letter. We are sure Dregus will be of great help to you in this quest. You are allowed one guest to accompany you. You must tell no one of your quest beside the mentioned, or your ownership will be null in void.

Sincerely,
First Chancellor Laymaine

Dregus's voice spoke again, "Ah, yes. I almost forgot about that. Human ownership is only half of this home. This journey is up to you. You can walk away now. If you do, I will erase every detail of magic from your mind. If you choose to undertake this task, then you will become the most powerful practitioner of magic on earth. So what will it be – magic or no magic?"

I thought for a second and then said, "My grandfather left me this house, so if I have to do this to keep the house, then I will do it."

Dregus chuckled again. "Well then, boy, you should get some sleep tonight. Tomorrow will be a very long day. I will do all I can to keep you on track, but this is all on your shoulders. Now go get some rest. I'll leave you be with your own thoughts the rest of the night."

Following his advice, I headed to my room. Sleep came easier than the night before. The cool night air blew me into my dreams.

CHAPTER II

The Tour

I AWOKE the next morning to a still house. It was so quiet that you could hear a pin drop. I got up from bed, brushed my teeth, and made myself breakfast. When I was almost finished with my meal, Buttons turned up. He had on his outfit from the night before, including his sword.

As I shoveled the last of the eggs into my mouth, Buttons said, "So, Alex, you ready for your tour of the grounds?"

After finishing the last of my orange juice, I said, "Sure, but how big is this place, anyways?"

"Human measurement, it's about seventy square acres of mostly forest land. Your grandfather acquired the land in an auction some years before the accident that claimed your parents' life," Thomas explained.

I paused to think. I responded with "So, my parents knew about this place."

Thomas stayed silent for a while. He took his nutshell hat off and wore a solemn look for a minute. Then he put the hat back on and said, "Let's get going, my boy. There is a lot to show you."

I walked over, picking him up and placing him on my shoulder. Thomas squirmed the whole time saying, "What do you think you're doing, you behemoth. Don't go around picking brownies up. It's undignified!"

Once on my shoulder, he sat cross-legged wearing a grim look. "You have been through most of the inside of the house, so let's go outside," Thomas grumbled.

So I walked through the front door, onto the porch. The sun was high in the sky. Its light blinded me for a moment as the world came into focus. The front yard looked wild from years of neglect. The rosebushes that lined the front porch were nothing more than a nettle of thorns. The two sentinel lawn gnomes that marked the front corners of the porch were smashed. Just shells of their feet remained. The old bird feeder – now yellow and overgrown with long stalks of grass – swarmed with the sound of insects, their wings beating the blades of grass.

"This is the front yard which was under the control of the fairies, but they seem to have disbanded since your grandfather passed. There is a lot of that around here. Most of the contracts are broken with his death. The fairies were in charge of maintaining the beauty of the area surrounding the house within one hundred feet of the foundation on all sides. Do you want to do something about it now or later?"

I stood looking at the yard I used to play in when I was young. I remembered Grandpa's vegetable garden. I walked off the steps and around to the left side of the house; about halfway from the front was a large fenced-in area with rotten tomatoes lying on the ground.

"He always took pride in this yard's beauty," I said. "How do we fix this, Buttons? My grandfather is rolling in his grave right now with the state of this property."

Thomas laughed and said, "Yeah, I would think so."

Thomas stood up and pulled out a silver-and-gold flute. Pressing it to his lips, he played a melody that reminded me of a spring breeze. When he stopped playing, the buzzing from the bird feeder grew louder. Spinning around, I stared in awe as the feeder started glowing yellow. The insect swarm buzzed faster and louder until the event came to a halt suddenly. The light faded, and the swarm disappeared. A large bird with green and gold feathers hovered over the pool of water.

At least, I thought it was a bird until it dashed in my direction, coming to a stop just in front of where I was standing. When the bird came closer, I saw that it was not a bird but a tan-skinned woman clad in a forest-green dress. Hanging from the bottom was an emerald the size of a pine cone. The green and gold feathers of the wings protruding out of her back beat the air gracefully, under which was a tattoo of webbed lines. The form I couldn't see because of the jet-black hair that hung infringed over her right eye. The left eye, which was visible, had an almond shape accompanied with chocolate-brown iris. If she were human, I would have said she was Native American or from some island country.

When she spoke, her voice was like the smell of flowers in a spring wind. "What is the idea of summoning me like a common fairy? Who is your company? Are you going to be true to your station, or will I have to lower myself?"

Buttons's face turned red as he spoke. "Alexander Gates, let me introduce the princess of fairies, Ms. Sabrina Windgreen."

In midair, she grabbed the waist of her dress and tilted her head.

"So this is the young one that Zavies left in his stead. Well, I guess you would like to make a contract with the fairies. You can present me with your terms. I'll relay them to the Queen, and we will either approve or deny them." Sabrina finished speaking.

I responded, "Can't we just go with the terms you had with my grandpa?"

Sabrina scrunched her nose then said, "You don't know the previous terms, so how could you uphold your side? No, you will give us your terms. Tomorrow, you will get your response from the Queen."

I thought for a moment then asked, "What were the conditions of the original contract?"

At that, Sabrina fluttered over to the porch banister and landed. The jewel at the bottom of her dress swung in the wind. I noticed the emerald-toed shoes peeking from under her dress line. "Well, Mr. Gates, what is that you would like us to do?"

She paused to wait for my response. I started by saying "Could you keep the area surrounding as you did for my grandfather?"

Thomas cut me off by saying "They were our scouts too. That Claus has served well in dire situations. I'm sure they knew Lucius was on his way."

"Now is that what brownies do, blame there inadequacies on other. As the lord of your people you should have a little more class." Sabrina said with smirk. "Your Queen has more tack than you when it comes to negotiating. You would do well not to insult me or my people." Thomas's face grew harder than usual. "Is this what it has come to sir? A War between Sprits, my Queen won't take too kindly to that. Fine we will retain our duties as scouts. Any other demands Thomas? "She said looking slightly put out.

"Now princess don't act so down, this is for the best for all parties involved." Thomas said returning her smirk. "If that is all then we have our own demands." Sabrina's zest started coming back to her. "For our services past, present and future, we the fairy's would like a section in the house library. The brownies have their own as protectors of the house. It's only natural that we have one as well." Thomas looked as if he wanted to say something but I cut him off by saying "I will agree to your terms but I wish to hold the right to adjust the contract as the need arises."

"I can't see why my Queen won't agree to these terms. You young sir are a good negotiator. I will speak with you tomorrow about your confirmation." When she finished speaking she flapped her wings and took off for the bird bath. When she was hovering over it, a light blinded me for a second. When it had faded she was nowhere in sight. Thomas stood on my shoulder muttering incoherently under his breath.

CHAPTER 12

Dante's Den

WHEN the yard was quiet again Thomas said "OK, next stop the kennel. It's in back of the house, just after where the fairy's defense line ends." I turned around walked past the vegetable garden. The smell of rot filled the air. Just as Thomas said after reaching the back of the house there was a large field. Just after that was a structure about 200 yards from the house. From where I stood all that could be seen was a large steeple. The rest of the building was lost in the trees. Thomas pointed at it and said that's where we are going. Following his directions it took twenty minute to reach. As it came into view, a large man was chopping wood. With a final swing he wedged the ax in to a tree stump he was using for a cutting board. As we walked up, he stretched his body to his full height. He raised his larger hands, waiving. The gruff in his voice harsh in the air "welcome young man. I take it you're the new master of grounds."

Thomas still on my shoulder shouts "hay Wolfman. How long has it been? All is well I hope." the man responded back "yeah, all is well Buttons. These dogs are keeping especially busy because of the approaching full moon." Wolfman strode to me and reached out his hand" His hair was sandy brown parted in the middle and Hung greasy around his jaw line. He wore a silver cross around his neck. He had a white button-up shirt with no sleeves. Both arms from the bottom of his elbow to the top of his wrist there were five leather belts, each strapped side by side down the length. He had on a pair of black work pants with worn black work boots.

When I grasped his hand, he said, "I'm Dante Wolfman. My job is to keep the pack in line." He shook my hand.

"I'm Alexander Gates. It is nice to meet you," I said in response.

A smile spread across his face. "Jaynes's second grandson – you're a good choice as caretaker. Most of the residents liked you as a child, so the transition should go smoothly. Why don't you come inside and have a drink with me?"

As we walked to the building, I asked Thomas, "Did he call you *Buttons?*"

He answered, "Yes, it's my middle name. I like it better than Thomas. That sounds too official. You can call me that, if you don't mind."

I smiled and said, "If you want."

Looking at it up close, the building was an old white church. The paint was graying with dirt and chipped in some places. We walked through a set of double doors in the front. The room I entered was once a congregation room. While some of the pews that lined the room were usable. Most were smashed or broken. The only thing intact was the large golden cross on the back wall. Even that lay slanted on the wall. There were two doors to the far left and right of the old pulpit. Lying across the foot of each door, were large gray wolfs sleeping on separate piles of clothes.

When we closed the door the one to the left of the cross jumped to his feet. Its eyes bounced from me to Dante and back for a moment. Then Dante said "It's OK Nala, young Alexander here has taken owner ship. Go spread the word." the wolf appeared to nod its head. Then took off through the door it was laying in front of. During this Exchange the other wolf lifted his head at the sound of my name, looked around, flicked its ears and lay back down. Dante turned his words to me saying "so I guess you are here to renew our contract. That you don't have to worry about, we can keep the same terms. We were responsible for roaming the grounds and keeping the peace. Kind of like internal police, we will report directly to you and no one else. All we require is free reign over the non-magical game on the land. Will you accept our conditions?"

Thinking to myself "this is not a bad agreement." Then from the back of my mind Dregus's voice spoke. "I can foresee a problem. My advice is to allow them rain over the smaller game. There are others that require a food source above all other things." Taking Dregus's advice, I relayed the message to Dante, and he agreed with the change. Just then a wild wind blew the door open from the outside. It startled me and Dante, but Buttons seem to be expecting it. A thunderous deep roar rang through the air. The entire church shook causing a few windows to shatter in. I looked at the doors as something slammed hard against them. I looked at Dante, his face looked slightly worried. Then I felt Buttons pat my cheek and said "Don't worry my boy, this is mostly for show. Although I think I should have introduced him be for I did Dante. It would have saved me a headache."

A loud voice came through as loud and deep as the roar. "Thomas, you dare to introduce the Keeper to this pack of mongrels before we, the thunder of Gatesholm. I will not stand for this insolence." The voice ended, and the door shook again.

"Buttons, you know we're ready for a good fight, but I think you should take the boy outside for now. We will be here waiting for your return. Our contract was never ended, we just adjusted it," Dante said with a smirk.

"We shall return. He might be with us as well," Buttons said, pointing at the door.

Much to my displeasure, we headed out. I thought this creature must be truly powerful if a werewolf is shaken up. The air was still and quiet, like after a really big storm. The only noticeable change outside was an imprint in the ground. It was large enough to fit two six foot tall slender built men lying side by side. It looked slightly like a dinosaur foot prints I seen at a history museum. Buttons stood tall on my shoulder and said "Here we are he who is named sightless death. At your request we present ourselves. Yet you remain unseen, would you be so kind." the air blew around us. Buttons dropped to his knees grabbing my shirt to keep from being blown off.

"Don't be petulant, I will appear shortly." the same voice as before said softer but still as deep. The air above the imprint started to shimmer like light off of a mirror. First a talons dug in the dirt appeared. Next the whole front foot, then a knee cap. Lastly, his hip came into view. After his dramatic revel, a majestic silver dragon towered above us. He could have easily dipped his head and swallowed me in one bite. The top of his head had three horns that looked like a crown. One in the middle of his brow pointed to his tail. The other two pointed to the sky. His pearly white teeth were the size of my entire leg. One of his eyes had the diameter the same as my height. His body was in the least as big as two houses if not more. If he were to spread his wings it would shade an entire city block.

He wore a bemused smile as he gazed at my awe struck face. "Close to the expression I was expecting but yours has more energy" a laugh trickled out. "I take it that I am the first true dragon you have seen? Let me introduce myself I am lord Arin, King of the Gatesholm thunder. I of course know who you Alexander, Zavies Gates youngest grandson. It would be my pleasure to have you join my thunder for our evening meal. Thomas knows the place. We will take care of our contract then. As for now I have other pressing matters to attend to. Farewell Master Alexander."

He leaped into the air, and with three flaps of his enormous wings he disappeared over the forest. Buttons waited a while before saying "let's join Dante and his pack." On our way back to the church, a large brown wolf with white on its snout came jogging past with three rabbits couched in its mouth. Nodding its head as it darted through the open door. We entered just after. Inside Dante sat gutting the hares that the wolf just brought in. He had on a smock smeared in blood. He looked up as we drew close and said "Rameau just brought us some dinner. I'll finish cutting it up later, let's head down to the kennel." he stood up and wiped his hands on the smock. Then took it off and laid it down on the stool.

He turned and walked to the door on the left side. He paused to scratch Nala, who had taken her place as sentinel once again. Continuing on, he walked down a flight of stairs just inside the door. As we made our decent, the smell of wet fur and blood filled the passageway. After twenty stairs, I stepped onto earthen floor. There was another door three feet away. The hall was lit by torches. It felt like walking through a mine. The next room was a large twelve foot square. All around the walls, there were cave like structure dug in. These seem to act as dens for the pack. There were at least 20 dens around this room.

In the middle of the room was a large fire pit. The smoke was channeled up through a grate in the ceiling. Set on the far wall was another hall. Most of the dens were empty, but about six of them had little cubs playing. Dante walked the length of the room with us in tow. The next hall only took about forty paces before then branched off into two other tunnels. Dante took the left path. As I passed by a breeze of fresh air blew from the right. Traveling down the tunnel, we came to another door. Dante unlocked it and waived us in.

Inside was a six foot by six foot room. Across from the door was a pile of four or five mattresses. On top were a tangle of blankets and a pillow. To the left of the bed was a wooden table whose legs were knarred as if chewed by something. To the left of the door was a large chest of drawers. Atop was a dragon skull, although not nearly as large as Arin. Once we were in Dante close the door, walked over and sat in a chair near the table. He must have noticed the way I was looking at the skull. So he said "To answer your questions, yes that is a dragon skull, killed it myself. Arin has not been in here so he does not know it's here." A smirk touched the crease of his lips. Buttons said, "Dante was an experienced hunter before he and your grandfather met. Although I didn't know this was here. If Arin finds out about this, there will be hell to pay."

It was quiet for a little bit, then Dante said, "I guess he can't find out." Then he let out a doggish laugh.

"Dante, why do the wolves listen to you?" I asked. The question seems to catch him off guard. When Dante started to answer, Buttons said "Dante is one of the few werewolves" on the land. In fact he is there leader. The wolves understand him because of what he is. They consider him there alpha." When Buttons finished speaking, Dante laugh loudly. "I couldn't have said that better." I thought of a number of other questions I wanted to ask but Dregus's voice rang in my mind "I will tell you all you want to know later don't pester him with questions"

Buttons looked at his wrist and said "oh my, it is getting late. We shall come another time. We have one more stop to make." Dante shook his head in acknowledgement then said "we shall be in touch. We have much time in which to spend with each other, so until then so long." Dante accompanied us back to where the hall split and said "if you take the right tunnel. Your next stop shouldn't be too far off." as he extended his hand. I grasped it and shook it gently. Torches flickered on the walls as we walked down the long tunnel. The air was still, after a few minute a light in the distance started as a pin prick. Then gradually grew to an exit for the cave. Just outside a forest stood. A few birds flew from tree to tree chirping. Buttons instructed me down an unseen path in the trees. The over growth masked the worn path making it hardly visible. As we walked, deer darted ahead startled by our approach.

The sun started to set, bringing a chill to the air. Minutes passed as the stars came out from hiding. The night air cold was against my face as I walked on. Finally we came to the side of a cliff. The land mass was as taller than nearby trees. From the bottom it looked flat on top. Buttons voice broke the silence "this is dragon's plateau. The land was raised with magic especially for the dragons. It has to be about ten miles around.

Just then, I heard a screeching chirping at the bases of the rock face. There was a large berry bush. Its berries gleamed red in the moonlight. Stepping toward the bush, it shook violently. The shrill grew louder the closer I came. The shaken bush tossed its fruit around the ground. I crouched down and separated the brambles. Near the center, I could make out a small pink form.

"I think it's a pig stuck inside," I said while reaching in further. Buttons ran down my arm and disappeared inside.

Moments later, I heard a cooing sound emanating from within. Buttons's voice came to me saying "Don't reach in anymore, this is not a pig. I will free it."

Then came the sound of a sword being freed from the scabbard. Sticking my head into the thorny brush, I watched as Buttons swiftly – and with precision – sliced through all the stems. I lost sight of him as he worked his way around the animal.

CHAPTER 13

Dragon Royalty

A LITTLE while later, the sound of Buttons's sword returning to its sheath signified his completion. "Step back I'm going to help her free," he said.

I took a few steps back, then the bush shook, and a pink dragon jumped out with Buttons between her shoulders. Her wings were small and folded to her back. Her tail twitched like a cat in the dirt. Buttons sat just behind her small crown. He gripped two of her three horn nubs to steady himself on her back. The little dragon couldn't be any bigger than a medium-size dog. Buttons rubbed the middle of her head, and she purred softly. Then he stood up and said, "Your hand, sir."

When my hand was in range, Buttons jumped onto the tips of my fingers. Walking back up my arm, he sat on my shoulder once again.

The little pink dragon sat watching the whole time. When Buttons was in position, he said, "So, Rose, how did you get stuck like that?"

The little dragon looked up, blinked her round emerald-green eyes, and said, "I came down here to practice hunting. I chased a rabbit into the bushes. Then I got stuck, and it ran away. That was this afternoon. My parents must be worried."

In a cheerful tone, Buttons said, "We are heading up there now. Would you like to accompany us?"

Rose did a little turn to express her excitement then said in the cutest tone while batting her eyes, "That would be great, Mr. Buttons. Who is this you are with?"

"My lady, I must offer my apologies for this rudeness. Alexander Gates, Keeper of Gatesholm, this is Lady Rose, princess of Gatesholm thunder. She was the first dragon to hatch here."

Rose bent her head in a bow and said, "It's a pleasure to make your acquaintance." After she lifted her eyes and met my gaze, her innocence could be seen in her stare. It filled my being with warmth.

"Well, gentlemen, why don't we get going? I'm sure my father is waiting for you guys." She turned and began to trot away. "If you don't hurry, you're going to have to deal with Scar on your own. Sometimes he is impossible," she said with a grin full of white teeth.

She headed down a path humming a tune. This trail was clearly tracked by dragons. It was at least as wide as a street. All the foliage was cut back at least two feet, leaving a grassy field. The path ran along the side of the rock face until coming to a large cave. The opening had to be at least fifteen feet high and equally wide. The air at the mouth smelled of grass and flowers – uncharacteristic of what I thought caves would smell. Rose disappeared inside. Her humming bouncing off the walls as we followed. The sounds of water dropping from the ceiling echoed as they hit hidden pools on the floor. As the mouth of the cave dwindled from sight, we came to a large wrought-iron gate in the middle of the passage. Rose sat on her hind legs in front of the bars, her tail twitching in the dirt.

"What are you doing?" I asked.

Her reply was as if stating the weather: "Waiting."

I walked up to touch the place where it parted. A pair of dark red eyes gleamed from the darkness beyond. Then a stream of thick smoke blew through, causing me to choke and stagger back.

A deep voice boomed powerfully through the cave. "Buttons, what is your reason for bringing this human here? It better be good, for you and your company will line my second stomach if not."

Buttons straightened his shirt and stood tall. I could feel his legs shaking, yet his voice did not when he said, "Scar, we were on our – "

Rose cut him off. "Scar! You will allow us entry or my father will have something to say about it."

A gust of air blew through the gates. Then Scar spoke in an attempt of sounding polite. "Oh, princess, I didn't see you there. So you will vouch for these two? You know my job. I'm not responsible for anything they might do within."

The eyes disappeared, and the gate swung open. Rose stood up and proceeded through. I followed along with Buttons on my shoulder. Just past the gate, a noise made me glance to my left. In the darkness, I could make out the same two red eyes and a set of large sharp white teeth showing underneath. The floating features were slightly disturbing.

"I take it that you're the new Keeper then. I am Scar the Unseen. Pleasure to meet you. Better hurry before I get hungry," Scar said with a chuckle.

I quickened my steps to catch up with Rose, not wanting to be left behind. On our way to her, Buttons mentioned something about Scar being all bark and no bite.

When we reached Rose, she was approaching the end of the hall; it turned into a huge cave. The walls towered like skyscrapers, high enough that there were wisps of clouds inside. Yet they didn't meet to form a complete roof. There was a hole large enough to slip a football stadium through. The whole structure looked as if a forest had sprouted inside a dormant volcano. The area closest to the end of the tunnel was a grassy field for about a mile. Then trees blocked the view forward from where I stood. When we were about halfway across the field, a breeze picked up, blowing the loose dust and leaves around. The wind sounded like someone beating a drum slow and steady. *Thump. Thump. Thump.* Just ahead of me, Rose froze in her tracks. Her head darted up into the sky, her neck twitching left and right.

As I looked to see what she was searching the air for, a large purple dragon came swooping down, hitting the ground in front of Rose. It let out an earsplitting screech, causing Rose to cringe and curl up in a ball. The larger dragon then turned its attention to me. Letting out another roar, it fell to its knees. The scales all over the creature body began to give off a purple gas. Its immense figure started to vanish into the thick cloud. The smoke compressed quickly with a blinding purple light. A dark-haired woman wearing a violet dress coalesced. On her feet were rounded toed shoes with no heel. She walked over to me extending her hand and said, "I would like to thank you for your assistance to my little Rose. My Name is Ladonna of Poison, Queen of Gatesholm's Thunder. My husband has told me all about you, Mr. Gates. Would you do me the honor of joining my family for dinner?"

I reached out and grasped her hand. Her fingers felt frail, but her grip was strong. Surely she could crush my hand with little effort.

Dregus's voice spoke in my head, "Don't let your mind be fooled by what your eyes can see. Even in human form, dragons are still quite powerful. However, with Ladonna, her strength is just secondary. Her true power is her ability to create a multitude of toxins in her body."

As the last of Dregus's words went through my mind, I heard Ladonna's voice, yet her lips were not moving. "If it isn't Dregus, It has been too long. So this is your new student. Alexander couldn't ask for a better teacher."

Dregus chuckled and then said, "Lady Ladonna, now you know the rule. You didn't request to enter his mind."

I responded out loud without thinking, "I don't mind. She seems nice."

This startled Buttons, causing him to flinch slightly. He said, "Don't mind what? What's going on? If I am present, I want to be involved."

Ladonna smiled while glancing at Buttons. "I didn't notice you there, Buttons. It seems time has treated you well. Can the same be said of your kin?" she said to him.

Buttons said, "My family is faring well. We have been keeping watch, as I'm sure you are as well."

Ladonna waited for Buttons to finish speaking. She then motioned for Rose to come over. Once she was within distance, Ladonna reached out and touched the little dragon on the snout. "You know better than to leave our coves like that. Humans are not to see you in your true form. Our presence here is one of the greatest secrecy. I won't have my own fledgling destroying our contract here," Ladonna scolded.

When she finished speaking, she released the little dragon.

The moment she did, the little dragon's form disappeared in a pink cloud. The cloud collapsed on itself, causing a flash of pink light. There was a brunette girl no older than six that stood where once a little dragon was. The little girl had a hot pink sundress with straps over her shoulders. The bottom was trimmed in silver and gold twined together. On her feet, she had pink sneakers with mismatched laces.

Ladonna looked at the little girl then said, "That's better. Now let's head to our den."

Ladonna took the lead. Rose followed close behind, with her head looking at the ground. I walked close enough not to get lost as we entered the forests. There was a trail wide enough for us to have tracked side by side.

After a few bends, Ladonna said, "There are hundreds of dragons that live in this forest. Most are watching us but wish to remain hidden. It is because of your grandfather that we are here. He took us in as refugees. To those who know of magic but cannot wield it, we are nothing more than beasts of burden, but with military applications. Zavies arranged it so that we could live here.

"Zavies listed this land as a nature preserve in the records of the United States. The information is also in a tome at the magical council's chambers. There is a scroll that cannot be opened by anyone since it has been there. Its label says 'for your eyes only' – yet it can't be examined. Your grandfather was very skilled at whatever magic he used, yet no one had ever seen him use any. Even in a situation when he was bound and gagged. Magic would just happen around him to his advantage. I never even felt any manna consumption from him. He would have to be the most extraordinary human I knew. You should feel proud to follow in his footsteps."

We crossed the entire hollow in a short time, coming to a lake set against the outer wall. High above, water fell from the opening in the rocky dome.

Ladonna turned to me and said, "This is the pool of our elders." She continued to speak as she led the path around the lake toward the waterfall. "Dragons grow in proportion to our age. Rose is but a hatchling, hence her human form appears as a child. I, who have lived more years than I care to share, look as thus – at thrice my age, I could easily fill half of this cave. There is a large population of dragons living here. So in a few decades, we would have far outgrown our home. Therefore, it was decided that when one reaches an unmanageable size, they would remove their heart from flesh and plunge it into the pool, giving our essence to all that dwell within this mound. For all life here drinks from this source. It is our way of returning to nature what we have taken over the years."

I asked, "Wouldn't that kill the dragon?"

Ladonna said, "Once removed, our hearts become a jewel in proportion to our size. Our consciousness and our magic are kept intact inside said jewel. Even though we have no physical body, it does not mean we are no longer able to wield magic. They are kept together here because to live eternity alone would drive anyone insane. I don't think you want a dragon going insane."

Ladonna finished speaking as the sound of the waterfall muted the world around us. We traveled along the edge of it where foliage met the clear liquid. At the cliff where the water splashed loudly, Ladonna placed her hand in the deluge, freezing it in midair. It looked like she had stopped time just for the water falling. The lake splashed and rippled. The water fell above us, but the water just where we were walking hung in the air.

Ladonna walked through the droplets, pushing them aside and leaving enough space so that I could walk through. I followed, careful not to encounter the droplets, not wanting to disturb the magic. Rose, however, started playing a game by pushing smaller ones together, making them larger. If she pushed the balls out too far, they would return to normal, falling into the lake and dissipating in its depths with a splash. Ladonna looked at her child. Letting out a chuckle, she beckoned her to continue following. We walked to the middle of the waterfall where there was an opening in the rock face.

I brought up the rear through the opening, the water resuming its thundering plummet behind us, creating a powerful torrent closing the tunnel. The sun filtered through the falls, lighting the passageway beyond. A ways down the hall, a large door stopped travel forward. It was all white, trimmed in gold and silver leaf patterns. No doorknob or a way to open it was present. Adorned in the center was a gold-and-silver nest as a knocker.

Something stirred inside the knocker as we neared. Ladonna spoke in a commanding tone, "Dar, wake and allow us entry. I of poison demand it."

Inside the gilded nest, a golden dragon no larger than my palm poked its head out. It spoke in a squeaky voice, "Yes, entry is granted to my queen." As the little dragon's head disappeared into the nest, the door folded in as if it were made of two distinct parts.

Through the door, we entered another cave, in the middle of which was a large gold-and-silver mansion. Ladonna led the way up to the door. The mansion couldn't hold a full-size dragon, yet humans could live comfortably inside. It was decorated in silver and gold from floor to ceiling. The quality of each item was exquisitely expensive. I thought to myself they must have more wealth then a medium-size country.

CHAPTER 14

Dinner with Dragons

LADONNA walked through the main hall with Rose and me just behind. We entered a giant dining room. The floor had golden tiles. Down the center of the room was a royal purple carpet. Set in the middle was a rectangular marble table with purple crystal chairs. There was enough seating for thirty people. There were two seats at each end and thirteen on each side.

At the head of the table, there was a blond man wearing a black suit with a white sash trimmed in gold, sitting in the right chair. He was conversing with two people. The man closest to him was very thin and bald. He wore large prayer beads around his neck and a red robe reminiscent of Tibetan monks. He sat silently.

The other person was a young boy no older than twelve. He had long unkempt black hair and dark skin. He wore a golden neck-and-wrist cuff with Egyptian hieroglyphs on them. His chest was bare, yet he had tarry cloth shorts with a belt that matched his cuffs. As we entered the room, his African accent could be heard over the other two voices. "You dragons think you're so powerful, but your power can't compare to mine. How do you think that you can stop pure evil, you weaklings!" the little boy's voice raged.

The man with blond hair stood up, slamming his hand on the table saying, "Of all the creatures of creation, we dragons are the form of power. We bore you and your tribe into the battle of angels. Yet you belittle my race by labeling us weak."

"Calm yourself, Azize. All will be as it should. We should not provoke our allies when we still have time," the other man said in a solemn manner.

The blond man sat down saying, "Ajhanon is correct. We have been friends since before Pangaea split apart. Our relationship is strong. We need to coexist as the few who know the great evil."

We came down the left side of the table, and Ladonna said, "Arin, how many times do I have to say no business at the dinner table?"

Arin looked up with a large smile then said, "I see you two have met our new Keeper. Alexander, I would like to introduce you to my other guest."

He gestured to the young boy and said, "This rambunctious youth is known as Azize, the heart of the mountain. The quiet monk next to him is the guardian Ajhanon."

Upon closer inspection of Azize, I noticed that he was slightly transparent with a blue haze around him. When he had seen me staring at him, he said with a gesture to himself, "Is there a problem? You don't want any of this?"

Ajhanon shook his head and said, "He is always full of energy. Don't be worried – we're all allies here. So Arin tells us that you're Zavies's youngest grandson. You have some grand shoes to fill, young one."

A large smile spread across Arin's face. "This boy is more than capable of fulfilling his duties."

Ladonna took the seat next to Arin, and Rose sat in the chair to her immediate left. So I took the seat next to her. As I sat down, three women came through a door behind Ladonna and Arin. Their facial futures were identical. All of them were dressed in French maid garb. The first woman was pushing a cart that had three large serving trays with tops on them. The second was also pushing another cart, yet her cart had a stack of golden plates, bowls, and cups. One of the cups had golden flatware. Next to that was a pile of white fabric napkins. The last woman had a cart as well; hers bore four pitchers filled with liquids of assorted colors.

The triplets went about in a flurry, distributing the contents of their carts. In a matter of minutes, the table was set and the ladies disappeared back through the doors from which they came. When the room returned to silence, Arin broke it saying, "So who would like to say grace? Alexander, would you please do us the honor."

Everyone's eyes turned to me, placing me on the spot. My mind frantically searched for the correct words. Then I remembered my grandfather. I said, "Everyone, bow your heads. Our Lord, we thank thee truly for the food we are about to receive. Also for the good health you have provided us. With the grace of our nameless Lord, Amen."

When I finished speaking, Arin clapped his hands together and said, "Let's eat." He reached for the platter in front of him, taking off the cover and revealing a pile of chicken pieces with the steam rising off in the shape of the lid.

Ladonna then removed another top to display a platter of baked potatoes, corn on the cob, and steamed carrots in a golden bowl. When the last serving tray was unveiled, there were condiments all arranged in their own small bowls.

Once all the food was displayed, Arin grabbed a chicken leg quarter and set it on his plate. Then, all at once, everyone else started to fill their plates. All except Azize – he sat with his plate empty, watching everyone take what they wished.

I looked over, asking, "Are you not hungry?"

Azize busted out laughing. Then he said, "It's obvious that you have much to learn. What you see is an astral projection. My true self is asleep, so I don't have to eat or drink." He picked up the plate in front of him, stuck it into his chest, then pulled it back out. "See? I'm not really here."

Ajhanon added a baked potato onto his plate of carrots. Afterward, he said, "I do not think this is the time for parlor tricks." Then he took an ear of corn.

Ladonna filled her glass with a glowing liquid then did the same to Arin's. Ladonna raised her glass and said, "To our new Keeper, may his life and health be great."

Everyone at the table raised their glass and spoke in unison, "To the Keeper." We all clinked our cups then took a sip.

My green liquid had the taste of apples and cinnamon. After Arin put his chalice back on the table, he said, "Shall we speak of our contract? All parties here are the only ones who know of our presence on this land aside from the Fairy Queen. Therefore our terms are that our residency remains secret. In return, we shall defend the air and ground herein. You can call any of our race brethren, and we shall do the same. Lastly, we request our word to be second to yours. Will you accept our terms, young Alexander?"

Buttons dabbed at his mouth with a small handkerchief and said, "So now you are using your contract to establish more power here. I won't stand for it. This land was created for equality amongst all residents. Zavies would be upset to see your grab at dominance."

A grin spread across Arin's face.

Then Azize said, "Such a loud bark from this small ant."

Ajhanon responded by saying, "We must not forget the story of the spider and the ant. A single ant is easy prey, yet the when outnumbered, the spider becomes the meal."

Through his smile, Arin said, "Our terms will not include your clan, Buttons. You shall remain as equals. It was meant for small squabbles over territory between our residents. We only wish for a peaceful existence. Ruling requires more than our secrecy will allow."

Everyone was silent until I said, "Lord Arin, I will accept your contract with one addition. I will reserve the right to change any decision I deem unjust. Do you accept?"

All were quiet then Arin said, "I will accept the Keeper's contract. Thank you, gentlemen, for witnessing our agreement." He gestured to Azize and Ajhanon. Then he continued to speak, "The hour grows late, so let us part with knowledge we leave as family."

Azize stood from his chair, saying with a smirk, "I hope you fare well on your mission, Lexxy." Then he clapped his hands together, and his solid body faded into his blue haze.

Then Ajhanon said, "Thank you for having me and my clan mate for dinner. And, Alexander, I shall see you soon." He then raised his hand to his nose and vanished in a flash of white light.

After Ajhanon's dramatic exit, Ladonna asked Rose to escort us to Scar's gate. Rose gave me a hug and a kiss then waved frantically as Buttons and I passed through the gate. Scar remained out of sight, yet I could hear the dragon's heavy breathing as we left the cave.

The night air was chilly as we made our way to the house. As we walked through a clearing, a pack of unicorns galloped out of the forest. The mass of white bodies looked spectral as the moonlight bounced off their collective hides. Near the old church, Dante was standing near the door, talking to someone who was concealed in the shadow of the building. Dante waved us over when I was close enough. Jayne stepped out into the light with a look of amusement on his face.

CHAPTER 15

My First Companion

JAYNES walk over, clapping his hands. "So you finally decided to get with the program. It took you long enough. I can see that Buttons is giving you the tour. How is Lady Ladonna? She was always nice to us growing up."

Buttons stood to his feet and waved to Jaynes as he addressed him. "How long have you know about this land?" I said, having trouble containing my shock of him knowing about magic.

His response was "Grandpa told me about this stuff when you were in grade school."

I stood there in shock, and then I screamed at him, "You know about all of this and never told me. Why? How? How could you not tell me? Especially after Grandpa died!"

Jaynes gave a mischievous smile and said, "Grandpa told me that you had to find out about this on your own – but when you did, you would need my help."

Dante stepped up and put his hand on my shoulder saying, "Calm yourself. All magical knowledge must be earned, nothing comes easy. If it did, then it would be worthless."

"So Dante tells me you're the new Keeper. Congratulations are in order, I think," Jaynes said.

Slowly I responded, "Yes, this is not fair. What else do you know? How come Grandpa told you?"

Jaynes responded, "Yes, Lexxy, I know about Dregus and your little ordeal. That's why I came tonight. I got a call from Dante here that you started making contracts, so I'm here to help."

Dante spoke up, "Your grandfather told me to do so years ago. He is to accompany you on your task."

Jaynes rested his back on the church wall and crossed one leg over the other with the smug look he always wore. This was the way he would stare at me when he knew something I didn't.

"Buttons, did you know about this?" I asked.

Buttons shifted his weight and said, "I was not aware of his role in your quest, but I was introduced to Jaynes when you were ten."

Then Dregus's voice spoke, "I knew as well, young one. His role is one of protection, as you have yet come to know your true power. He will be instrumental as you venture to lay claim to this land."

Jaynes unknowingly cut off Dregus and said, "Buttons, why you don't use the tunnels and head back to the house? I want to take him to the lake to complete the light contracts."

Buttons stood up and said, "I don't see a problem with that. Don't forget to contract Primus and his herd. They should be near the lake at around this time."

Silence ensued, then I asked, "What time is it, anyway?"

Dante replied, "Around three in the morning."

After exchanging good-byes, Dante and Buttons disappeared into the church. Jaynes and I took a path to the left of the church.

After a while, I started quizzing him again. "So how come Grandpa didn't name you Keeper? What else lives here? What did Grandpa teach you?"

I heard his chuckle ahead of me, then his answer drifted back. "There are creatures of light and dark that live here, as well as normal animals. You have already met most of the light creatures and one of the dark."

I spoke up again, not allowing him to answer the other questions. "Who was the dark creature?"

This time, he laugh loud for a second then said, "Dante is considered to be a dark creature. Even though his demeanor is nice, he is still a werewolf."

Confused, I said, "How does that make him a dark creature?"

Jaynes said, "A dark creature is considered such because they eat living creatures to survive."

He answered my question as we came into a grassy field with a large lake sitting still the middle. Crowded around the edge of the water were three men with fishing poles in the water. The dew-ridden grass mashed with every step we took. When we were about ten yards from them, the man in the middle turned his head and waved his arm in the air. His voice was deep yet tender when he spoke, "Hail to the grandsons of Zavies. What brings you two out on this early morning?"

Jaynes put his arm around my neck, pulling me into a headlock, saying, "Our little Lexxy has come to contract those that dwell in the lake."

I examined the trio. Their upper halves were those of men, yet at their waist down were those of stallions. All three had muscular brown skin; the man on the left had long black hair. It hung down his back. In contrast, the man in the middle was bald with a mustache. The one on the left was the youngest of the three. He had a short-cut fade and no facial hair to speak of.

Jaynes walked over and shook the middle centaur's hand then said, "This chestnut-colored gentleman is the leader of the herd."

The centaur reached out toward me. I grasped his hand and shook it gingerly. "My name is Primus. The young one to my right is my son Quentin, and my brother Jeffery. It is nice to meet you face to face, Keeper."

He released my hand and said, "Well, since we are here, let us make our contract. We, the Centaur herd of Gatesholm, will be your foot soldiers should you ever have need. We only require free roam of these lands. We don't claim one part of this land. Also, if you are in need of ethereal guidance, we will provide you the best we can. Will you accept our contract?"

He reached out his arm. I hesitated for a moment then grasped his hand.

Primus released my hand and grabbed my forearm saying, "This is how we seal our bond. It is a warrior's grasp."

With a smile, Jaynes chuckled in the background.

The trio of centaurs and Jaynes spoke for a while before they departed, leaving Jaynes and I alone with the still lake. Jaynes led me to the edge saying, "First, you need to call someone from below. Walk to the water's edge then plunge your head into the water and say 'I, the Keeper of Gatesholm, call to those who dwell in these depths.'"

Walking slowly, I did as he asked. After I said the line, I pulled my head up, gasping for air. Jaynes fell onto the grass, holding his sides with laughter. "I can't believe you still haven't learned that everything told to you may not be the whole truth."

"Your brother speaks the truth, Keeper. You did not need to submerge your head. You could have just called out," said a voice from behind me.

I turned to see a female's head bobbing in the water. Her hair was the color of seaweed, and her silvery blue eyes shined in the moonlight. The head floated toward the shore. Slowly it rose out of the water, displaying the rest of her body. She had on a short dress that came down to her knees, with one strap over the shoulder. The texture of the dress looked like fish scales. Her hands and bare feet were webbed between the digits, but otherwise normal. She walked up to me and did a little curtsy saying, "My name is Aquana, I am the Mere Queen's voice. Any dealings with land dwellers, I take care of on her behalf. I believe you came tonight to contract my people."

She continued to speak as she exited the water. "We only require the all water source remain under our protection and that they are not polluted in any way. If you can accept our terms, then we shall conclude our contract with a kiss."

She strolled to me, wrapped her arms around my neck, and pushed her lips against mine. A second later, she pulled away to the sound of Jaynes's laughter once again. Furious, I said, "What's so funny now?"

He simmered down and said, "How much trouble would you be in if Ontia had seen that?"

My face dropped at the thought of Ontia storming through the field and punching Aquana on her jaw. Aquana's voice broke my daydream.

"If that is all, my Keeper, then I'll return to my home before I dry out too much." With a smile, she dashed back to the water and disappeared into its depths.

When she was gone, Jaynes turned on his heels and led the way down the path. I followed closely behind him. As we turned past the church, toward the house, the sun started to peek out of the eastern horizon. Jaynes looked over his shoulder and asked, "So, Lexxy, what's for breakfast? All this meeting and greeting has given me an appetite."

Thoughts of bacon and eggs with a side of hash browns flicked in my mind. As I went to convey my image to him, a large black SUV sped down the driveway. It came to a stop near the front porch as we came around the side of the house. A tall slender man with blond hair in a black suit and shiny shoes got out. He straightened his suit and walked over to Jaynes and me.

"Good morning. I am looking for Alexander Gates. I am Special Agent Frisco with the Secret Intelligence Agency," he said while extending his hand toward Jaynes.

Jaynes took two steps back, almost bumping into me. I took his hand instead in a firm grip and shook it briskly. I said, "I am Alexander Gates. This is my brother, Jaynes."

Frisco gave me a friendly smile then said, "It's a pleasure to make your acquaintance. Would you please accompany me? My director would like to ask you a few questions. I don't think we will take too much of your time."

Jaynes looked at me and said, "I am going to go inside and make something to eat. I will be here when you get back." Backing up again, he turned and went into the house.

Agent Frisco went back to the truck. I followed him and sat in the passenger seat. The key turned, the engine roared, and we were off.

CHAPTER 16

SIA

WE drove the half hour to the city's downtown. There we went to a large building near the central library. Parking in the underground car ramp, we then took the elevator to the thirteenth floor. The door opened, and the few people who accompanied us from the parking lot got off. I went to exit the elevator when Agent Frisco grabbed my shoulder and pulled me back, saying we were on the next floor. The doors closed, and Agent Frisco pulled the STOP button out. Then he took out his keys and separated them to reveal a single black key hidden among the brass. He put the key to the button for the thirteenth floor. The key slid into the button as if it were an unseen keyhole. When he turned it, the doors opened again.

The floor we were on was not the same one the other people got out on. On the wall, there was a sign that read: "We guard what the world is not ready to know." Just above that were the letters on large bold print: SIA. Underneath sat a woman at a desk. She looked up when we left the elevator. Frisco walked up to the front of the desk and spoke to the woman.

Her squeaky voice said, "The director is waiting for you in conference room four."

Frisco said, "Thanks, Gina. Oh, also, could you tell Francisco I am back?"

Gina looked up and said, "I think he is in the bull pen with Tanya there about to head out on a mission."

He said good-bye to Gina, and we walked through a set of double doors. On the other side was a large room with dividers and desks. The air hummed with the flipping of papers and the scribble of ink pens. Telephones rang, people having conversations. The room was a bustle of activity. Agent Frisco led me down the left wall. We passed a couple of doors with numbers until he opened a door with the number 4 on it. He waved me inside then closed the door behind me. Seated at the head of a long conference table was a tall, fat, bald man typing on a laptop.

When the door closed, he looked up with a smile on his face and said, "Welcome, Mr. Gates, I am glad to see you could make it. Would you please take a seat, and we will begin."

As I took my seat, he pulled out a large black book.

"I am Director John Duncan. I am just going to ask you a few questions, and then you are free to go. I have known your grandfather for many years. He was an honorable man. He was my partner for many years before your father was born. As I understand, you are going to take ownership of his home. Have you contracted the other residents? Will they accept you as the new Keeper of the grounds?"

Before I began to answer his questions, Dregus's voice came into my head. "Be leery of this man. He may have been a friend of your grandfather's, but he is no ally of yours. I can sense a dark presence in him."

With Dregus's warning in mind, I answered his questions with caution. "Yes, I have done all in accordance with his will. Yet I didn't know there were other residents on the land."

He smiled and said, "Mr. Gates, I know what dwells beneath your land. The contracts are here for me to read. I know of the wolf pack and the fairies that are residents."

Again, I feigned ignorance in my answer. "I did see some wolves running through the forest – but, sir, do you expect me to believe that fairies exist? I am not a child, sir, so do not try to tell me fairy tales. I stopped believing those long ago."

The director's expression changed instantly. I could hear a tone of disdain behind his smile. "If you do not start answering my questions honestly, this process is going to take longer than it should. I am going to start to record your answers now. I implore you to answer truthfully."

He pressed the recording button in the tape deck sitting near the binder then said, "This is the formal inquiry of Alexander Gates in relation to his family's estate. Please state your name and that you consent to this process."

I waited a moment then said, "I, Alexander Gates, consent to the process of acquiring the property previously held by my grandfather Jaynes Gates Sr."

Director Duncan spoke again when I finished. "You, Alexander Gates, are responsible for care and maintenance of the house and the surrounding dwellings for up to seventy acres. You also have to pay any duties or taxies for said property. If this is acceptable, state yes and sign the forms here."

When he stopped speaking, he slid the forms across the table along with an ink pen. I scanned it quickly then said "I accept" and signed the bottom.

"Thank you for your time, Mr. Gates. I will have Agent Frisco take you back. You can wait for him at the receptionist desk," Director Duncan said while taking the forms I just completed.

I got up and walked to the door. Before I opened it, he said, "If I have any more questions, how would I contact you?"

I told him my phone number then walked out the door. He scribbled it down on the form I signed. As I walked out, I heard him whisper, "Yes, my lord. He denied all of said knowledge, as you said."

I leaned around and asked, "Were you talking to me?"

He looked up from his notes saying, "No, I was talking to myself."

I smirked, saying OK, and walked out.

Out in the office, Agent Frisco was standing with a beautiful blond woman and a Hispanic man with short black hair. They seemed to be deep in conversation. When I came into the room, Frisco waved at me. I pointed at the receptionist's desk, and he shook his head yes, and then went back to talking. I walked into the receptionist area and took a seat.

Agent Frisco came out twenty minutes later.

CHAPTER 17

Kidnapped

THE ride home was filled with small talk on various subjects. It felt shorter than when we left, yet it was the same distance traveled. I arrived home around noon, Jaynes car was still parked in the driveway. As Frisco pulled out of my driveway, I ascended the front stairs. As my key slid into the lock the wind kicked up. Then a thundering boom as the ground shook under the porch. I turned around to see Ladonna in dragon form breathing heavy. I heard the door open behind me and Jaynes's voice yelling, "What is going on?"

Ladonna changed into human form. Her clothes were ripped, and there were scratches across her cheek, which were bleeding heavily. Jaynes dashed off the porch in time to catch her as she fainted. We carried her into the living room, laying her on the couch. Jaynes went to the kitchen to grab some water and towels. I stayed with her until he came back. We cleaned her wounds and bandaged her up as best we could. She came to as we were cleaning the gash on her cheek. Frantically, she started saying, "They came and took her! They took my little girl. We couldn't stop them – you have to help me!"

"Slow down and start from the beginning. Who took Rose?" I said, trying to sound calm, but the thought of a dragon being kidnapped was weird. I thought to myself that dragons were at the top of the food chain.

After she calmed down, Ladonna began to tell the story slowly. "About two hours after you left, one of our century reported that a group of dark dragons were approaching. Arin and I took flight to intercept them. We dispatched the group with minor effort. What we did not notice were the few dragons that came on foot. By the time we made it back to our cove, Scar had been rendered unconscious. The rest of the guards as well, and Rose was missing. We only knew what happened after we were able to revive Scar. He had some major injuries, but nothing he can't heal from. Arin went after them, and I came here to tell you."

She stopped speaking and started struggling to breathe. Then her eyes rolled into the back of her head. Her body went limp, yet I could still see her chest rising. Jaynes and I exchanged looks of concern. Then a tiny voice from the mantel said, "Boy, what are you waiting for? There has been a breach of security. What are we going to do about it?"

I turned my head to see Buttons wearing army-green fatigues with his sword at his side. He pulled his sword from its sheath and thrust it into the air and yelled, "Mobilize the troops!"

Jaynes said, "Buttons is right. You should check to see what else is going on around here. There might be more dark dragons stalking the land.

I thought to myself, "What would Grandpa do?"

Dregus answered back, "You should send the brownies to have the wolves and centaurs check the grounds."

I repeated what Dregus said to Buttons, and he vanished behind Grandpa's wedding picture.

Jaynes put a wet cloth on Ladonna's forehead, and then covered her with a blanket. I asked Dregus, "Why are dragons kidnapping Rose?"

My mind was quiet for a bit then his voice answered, "They are called dark dragons because they have lost the ability to reason for themselves, leaving only a bloody primal nature. I have been in contact with Arin. He has told me that these dragons seem to be under someone's control. Who is controlling them is what we have to find out. Arin has asked if you could report this to the council as you have to go there, anyway."

Buttons came back a little while later saying, "The centaurs were unaware of the dark dragons, but Dante says that twelve wolves were injured in the western woods. They saw the dragons moving quickly off the land with Rose in one of their mouths. They attempted to stop them to no avail. The centaurs are patrolling all quadrants so the wolves can heal."

"I want you and Jaynes to come to the library. You will need something I have been keeping," Dregus said.

"Wait, Jaynes knows about you also? Why am I the last to know this?" I said, growing angry.

"Your brother knows of my existence, yet we have never come in contact. Since you have chosen him as your partner in your quest, he will need to hear what I have to say as well," Dregus responded calmly.

So I led Jaynes to Dregus's cave, where we found the dragon sitting cross-legged, sipping a cup of tea.

He started speaking as soon as we were in earshot. "Jaynes, I am glad we can finally meet, even though the conditions are not great. I know you know who I am." Dregus paused.

Jaynes looked the dragon over with an expressionless face and said, "You are the dimension dragon who holds this reality together. If you were to die or be captured by evil forces, all could be lost."

Dregus chuckled and said, "Oh, interesting use of the word *could be*. Let's get on track. I have brought you here to provide you with one of the few ways to travel to Subterra. This bracelet is for Alexander – to activate it you need sight of magic and a few molecules of water." Dregus handed me a bracelet made of silver with a blue gemstone in its center. "You need only speak the name of a place. This bracelet will absorb some water and instantly teleport you there."

Jaynes was given an onyx ring. "With this ring and a little mental discipline, you can make any object you can imagine. It uses the earth around you to power itself," Dregus spoke as he handed a golden ring with a large black stone in it. Then he said, "OK, Jaynes first. Put the ring on and create a something."

Jaynes slid the ring over his finger and made a fist, examining it. Then he bent down, putting the top of his hand to the ground. He closed his eyes then started to stand up. As he did, the dust swirled around his hand and he pulled a shining sword out of the dirt as if pulling it from a sheath.

Jaynes swung it around, cutting through the air. Dregus walked over, grabbing the blade with his bare hand. The blade crumbled to dirt at his touch. Dregus smiled, saying, "You just need to concentrate a bit more, but you seem to grasp the principle behind it. When you have mastered it, the items you create will become indestructible. Now, Alexander, all you need is a little water."

Dregus stamped his foot, making a deep imprint in the dirt. Then he waved his hand over the imprint saying "Aques." Water filled from the bottom up in the shape of his footprint.

I took the bracelet from Dregus and put it on. It turned into liquid then ran down my hand to my finger, coating my hand and forearm with a liquid metal. After it touched the ring, the metal hardened, and both jewels turned green.

Dregus smiled and said, "This gauntlet was created by your grandfather just for you. He broke it into different parts so as to not overwhelm you. Once it is fully assembled, it will help you to protect this land from even the greatest darkness.

"Now touch the surface of the water and say where you want to travel. To bring someone with you, keep them in mind when you say where you're going. For now, say 'mere pool, Gatesholm.'"

I did as he instructed and thought of Jaynes. The water raced up and down my body, encasing me. I had no trouble breathing when I looked over at Jaynes, who was encased as well. We were then sucked into the puddle. Seconds later, I felt webbed hands pulling me upward. Looking around, I saw Aquana swimming to the surface. To my side, Jaynes was being pulled by another mermaid with red hair.

CHAPTER 18

Brunch

WHEN we broke the surface, the cold air hit my face. The sun was high in the sky, clouds hiding it from view. The mermaids released us, and we swam to the shore. Aquana spoke as we trudged to the land. "How come you didn't appear closer to the surface? If the spell had worn out sooner, you could have drowned." She splashed backward and slipped underwater.

Dregus's voice spoke in my head, "More concentration would have placed you where you wanted to be. Yet that was good for your first attempt. You cannot use this method to enter Subterra, but it can take you to the outer caves. Now take what I have shown you and finish your quest."

Just as Dregus finished speaking, Ronan came galloping to us. He was moving so fast that he skidded to a halt, breathing heavily. He gathered himself and began to speak, "Keeper, all the dark dragons have either been dispatched or have fled the premises. Lord Arin was seen heading west in pursuit of the others. I am told that you intend to head to Subterra. Who will you leave in charge?"

I thought to myself that things were moving too fast. Dregus chuckled in my head and said, "That is the burden of leadership, to maintain control. Even while all else around is in chaos."

With Dregus's words in mind, I said to Ronan, "Ladonna is currently at my house. I will stay in contact with her. She will convey my thoughts if the need arises. She should be able to protect everyone while I'm gone."

Ronan nodded his head saying, "You are wise beyond your years, young one. We will abide by your words and hold true to our contract in your absence. Also, you seem to have two visitors sitting on the porch."

After our exchange, Ronan trotted off into the forest. Jaynes and I walked to the house to find Ontia and Nevalin sitting in the shade on the porch. They were deep in conversation; their laughter could be heard in the back of the house.

Nevalin was the first to see us when we were in sight. She leapt out of her seat and dashed over to Jaynes. Jumping on him, she wrapped her legs and arms around him. This made Jaynes stagger back slightly. She let go, falling back to the ground slowly.

Ontia stepped off the porch and wrapped me in a tender embrace. She kissed me softly on my cheek then said, "Nevalin and I are going to the movies and was wondering if you guys wanted to join us?"

Jaynes shook his head saying, "Sorry, girls, but Lexxy and I have a few things to take care of."

Nevalin shot him an upset look.

Ontia said, "Oh, it's OK. We will go ourselves. I hope you guys have a good time. Come on, Nevey."

Nevalin let out a sigh then said, "The movie doesn't start for another few hours. Can't we hang out for a bit?" She stopped talking and glanced at Jaynes.

Ontia saw it, smiled a little, then said, "I guess we could stay for a bit, as long as Alex says it's OK."

Nevalin gave me a pleading look. With a smile on my face, I said, "We can leave when you girls do. Would you girls like to have a bite to eat?"

Nevalin said yes, but Ontia said, "I'm not really hungry, but you can eat if you wish."

When I walked into the house, Ladonna shot up from where she was lying. She looked at me with a stern look and then walked into the kitchen, disappearing behind the door that led upstairs. I looked behind me to see Ontia and Nevalin standing in the doorway. I smiled and said, "Come in and make yourselves comfortable."

With that, Nevalin pushed past Ontia and sat on the couch. Ontia glided into the room, every step seemed to have purpose. Jaynes walked in, closing the door behind him. He sat next to Nevalin on the sofa. I walked into the kitchen and started to rummage through the cabinets.

"You need to go food-shopping, I see."

Ontia's voice made me jump. Almost dropping the box of pancake mix, I turned around to find her a step away from my face.

She giggled and kissed me on the lips. "How long were you there?" I asked.

She took the box out of my hand and grabbed a bowl. Then she said, "I followed you from the living room. I wanted to leave those two alone for a while."

She finished speaking while she poured the powder into the dish. She then added water and handed it to me. We continued quietly cooking the flapjacks. Every now and then, we flirted with each other until we were finished. All four of us sat down and enjoyed our brunch. Afterward, we sat in the living room making small talk.

Around six o'clock, the girls started gathering their things to leave. We escorted them out, standing on the stairs – watching them get into the car and pull off, leaving a dust trail billowing behind them. The car disappeared around a bend in the road, when a hand grabbed my shoulder firmly and pulled me into the house.

CHAPTER 19

Cave of Souls

WHEN my shoulder was let go, I was staring into Ladonna's face. She wore a look of concern. When she spoke, her voice seemed cautious. "Something is not right about those girls – those two smell of death. I could not tell you which one because their scent is intermingled. Dregus agrees with me, take care in dealing with them."

Her concern offended me. I shook my head saying, "I have known them for years. I met them in one of my college classes. Ontia and I have been dating since our junior year."

Ladonna sat on the love seat, crossed her legs, and said, "I am just warning you that they are not as they appear. Your sight hasn't revealed anything about them?"

I mulled over what she said. Then I said, "No, they look the same as when I first met them."

Ladonna sat back saying, "That could mean either they are human and I smell something else, or that their true form is humanoid. Either way, you should be careful."

In my head, Dregus's voice chimed in, "You should heed her warning, but now is not the time for contemplation. You and your brother should come to my den at once. The hour grows late. The time for your departure is at hand."

Ladonna shifted on her seat. Jaynes watched me in silence until I told him what Dregus had said. When I was done talking, he grabbed his coat and dashed upstairs. I went to follow him when Ladonna said, "Be careful. There are forces that would see ownership of this land taken from you. Do not fall prey to their deceptions. Go in peace, Alexander." After she finished speaking, she picked up the newspaper from the inn table and started to read.

When I walked into Dregus's den, he and Jaynes were speaking in a low tone. They stopped abruptly when they heard me come in.

"Now that you're here, we can get a move on. Jaynes and I were just speaking of your entry point near Subterra. It is inside the cave of souls. Use your ring like you did before, thinking of the surface of the pool of souls. Jaynes will show you the way after that. You won't need to bring anything else with you." Dregus stopped talking and walked over to his footprint filled with water.

I reached down into the water; the jewels glowed blue on my hand and wrist. When I felt Jaynes's hand press on my back, I spoke out loud, "Surface of the pool of souls." The water encased my hand, rushing up my arm like a river. A moment later, I felt the water being drawn into the footprint. It swept me off my feet like a wave at a beach. The world turned dark blue.

When I regained my footing, sounds of dripping water echoed around me. The air was damp, and the only light was coming from stalagmites standing two feet from me. Splashing from behind alerted me that Jaynes was making his way to the water's edge. I walked over to the lighted stone tower and touched it. It felt warm in my hand as opposed to the cold air. Looking around, I noticed there were many light sources scattered around the cave. The light even danced of the surface of the lake.

"Lexxy, come on. We don't have all day to sightsee," Jaynes yelled, disappearing into the mouth of a huge tunnel. I had just followed behind him when the hair on the back of my neck stood on end.

"Alexander, don't leave us. Come visit with us," a voice carried by the wind said.

I turned around, not seeing anyone. I shrugged and continued into the tunnel.

The wind rushed past me again, carrying the same voice. "Come back, we are so lonely. Stay awhile, chat with us."

I spun around quickly. There, floating in midair, was a woman I had never seen the likes of. She looked like Azize, yet more see-through. She never attempted to come into the tunnel, only floating at the mouth. Her face looked as beautiful as any cover-girl model. Yet her clothes were rags that floated in the air around her, like she was underwater. My foot moved toward her without me thinking of it. Then the feeling like I was missing something flooded over me, causing me to take another step toward her.

Her voice came again in the wind. "Yes, come to me, Alexander. Come keep me company." Her arms lifted up, beckoning me back.

I took another step toward the woman. Then I felt a hand on my shoulder. Then Jaynes's voice spoke, "Don't listen to her, Lexxy. Come on, we have to go."

I turned to face him, his voice seemingly breaking my trance. I felt Jaynes yank on my shoulder, pulling me deeper into the tunnel. When the distance increased from the mouth, the woman let out a shrieking "no, come back!" I turned to see her face had grown skeletal. Her eyes were sunken and void of an iris.

Jaynes tightened his grip and threw me to the ground. He bent down, placing his hand in the dirt. I looked back at the mouth; now there were more forms gathered, beckoning me back. Jaynes looked up at the mouth and a wall of earth shot up, closing the opening.

CHAPTER 20

Subterra

SEALED inside of the tunnel, the pull of the specters was lost. Jaynes grabbed me by my arm and pulled me to my feet.

"What was that?" I asked as he started to walk away.

"Dregus warned me about the wraiths that guard the pool of souls. If you went back, they would have fed off your soul until you turned into one of them. We need to keep going this way," he said as he walked ahead of me.

"But why was I the only one affected?" I asked, trying to keep up.

"I don't have an answer to that, but lucky I was here or else you would have been their next meal," he said, chuckling as he walked.

We had walked about a mile when I noticed two doors made of oak blocking the way forward. Jaynes and I stood staring at them. The doors were rounded at the top, yet there was no handle to open them. Jaynes walked forward, placing his hand on the left door. Then he put his shoulder against it. I could see the strain in his body as he tried to open it. He tried for about five minutes and stepped back.

"I can't believe we made it all the way here and can't open some doors," he said as he threw a rock at it. The rock bounced off, clattering to the floor. He started pacing back and forth. "I can't believe you got me here and don't even know how to get in," Jaynes said angrily.

He walked up to me and shoved my shoulders. I stumbled back, only catching my balance on the side of the tunnel. I charged him with all the force I could muster. He dodged out of the way, leaving his foot to trip me as I passed.

I stumbled forward, but both my hands landed on the doors, balancing me out once again. I went to pull away from the door, yet I could not. My hand passed into the door, making a sucking sound. I yelled for Jaynes to help me. I felt him wrap his arms around my waist, pulling with all his might. With every yank, I sank deeper into the door. I could hear him yelling "no, no, no" as we both were pulled completely inside.

It felt like being hit with thousands of blunt toothpicks. I tried to move but couldn't even shift one finger. I called out to Jaynes, only to hear my voice muffled. Then I heard footsteps in front of me. Then a gruff voice said, "You bumbling piece of wood, let them free!"

There was a knock, then light blinded my eyes as I fell forward. My face hit a cold, smooth surface, then the air was knocked out of me when something fell on top of my back. I opened my eyes to see green-and-white tiled floor pressed against my face. The same gruff voice asked, "Are you two going to lie there all day? I do believe you have a meeting to attend."

The weight shifted off my back, and I heard Jaynes say, "Haven't seen you in a while, Fate. How is your little girl?"

I stood up on my feet; Jaynes was embracing a man cloaked in a dark blue robe with the hood pulled up. They parted, and the man said, "It is a pleasure to meet you, young Gates. I am the ursa mage – Fate." He extended his arm. Protruding at the end was a bear paw covered in black fur. His claws were long and yellow, with a slight curve at the tips.

I shook his paw with a slight apprehension, causing Jaynes to chuckle. "Don't you remember Mr. Benjamin, Lexxy?"

Then realization set in. I asked, "The same Mr. Benjamin that came to Grandpa's parties! He was a black man, not a bear."

Fate let out a grizzly laugh. "Not used to your new sight yet. What you see now is my true form. This appearance would cause quite an uproar if norms were to see me. So to venture into their world, we showcase a look that's pleasing to their eyes. If you gentlemen would follow me, the council members are waiting."

He turned and started walking down the hallway. I followed Jaynes as he walked next to Fate. They started talking about Fate's little girl and wife.

As we strolled, I noticed there were pillars lining the walls. Hung between them were large paintings with ornate frames. Each was different. There was one of a man sitting in a tall thronelike chair. Another showed a field with unicorns dashing through. Yet another displayed a battle between werewolves and vampires.

Fate looked over his shoulder and said, "These show either important events or people in magical history."

The hallway ended in another set of oaken doors. Fate pushed them open, and we all waked through.

We entered a massive cave, inside of which was a sprawling town of adobe houses made of green glass. A golden bricked road led down the center of town, ending at a large lake in the center of town. As we walked through, I noticed that the green glass was, in fact, crystallized Jade. The town was abuzz with residents shopping at the stores along the main road. It was like a small city inside of a cave.

Fate led the way through the crowded street. A multitude of stores had their wares out for show. The shops had a variety of goods – one with food and herbs, another with clothing. I even saw a store with a sign that read "a free potion with every purchase." There was a pet shop with cages stacked in the windows. They contained an assortment of creatures. Cats, dogs, birds, and even bats – but there were animals I had never seen also. I watched a little boy exit the shop with a lizard sitting on his shoulder, its whole body flaming.

We made our way down through the town to the lake's shore. The beach was just as lively as the town, with children building castles in the sand and swimming. Fate stood at the water's edge, staring out. Kids were darting back and forth from the water. Suddenly, the middle of the lake started to bubble like a pot on a stove. After a minute, a single crystal tower rose from the froth. Water poured off it as more towers sprouted. Then I realized what was happening. A glasslike castle rose from the depths of the lake. We stood and marveled at this water-born structure for a minute.

Then fate looked at me and said, "This is the first time you have seen the Crystal Citadel. Its ascension is a sight to behold. It is made out of dragon glass. It is one huge piece. But enough with our small talk – they're waiting for you."

CHAPTER 21

The Council of Antiquity

FATE stepped off the beach, and instead of splashing into the water, he started to walk on top of it. He casually walked five steps and looked at our astonished faces. He waved his hand for us to follow him. Jaynes and I looked at each other then I went forward. The sensation was like walking on a water bed. Jaynes and I followed Fate atop the water. With every step I took, the thought of falling in came to mind. The children swimming did not even take notice of us, except one girl who swam up to me and tried to hand me a clump of seaweed.

Our wet track only took a few minutes until we were staring at the crystalline walls of the castle. Fate put his hand on the wall and said out loud, "Fate the mage request entry for himself and two guests." Then, where he placed his hand glowed white, and then extended down to the water level. It expanded to the size of Fate and a voice said "access granted."

Fate looked over his shoulder saying "Shall we go?" as he disappeared into the light. I put my hands in front of me and walked forward into the light.

I entered a long white marble hallway. Golden chandeliers hung at the ceiling, lit with candles. Their flickering flames made shadows dance on the tiled floor. There were painted portraits hung along the walls, each of a different person seated in the same golden throne. Fate saw me admiring them and said, "This is the Hall of Portraits. Those depicted are the twelve members of the Council of Antiquities." As we walked, he would point and say their names.

The first on our left was of Gruff the Stout, the dwarves' representative. He stood in front of the throne with his foot planted on the head of a war hammer, the shaft of which extended higher than he himself stood. On the opposite wall hung loony Frigeo, the shifters' representative – his face half concealed by a matted black beard and mustache. Next to him was Arin, the dragon representative. He looked the same as when I had met him at home. Across from Arin was a short slender woman with flaming red hair. Her face looked young except around her eyes. That looked older than the rest of her. Fate said that she was Laymaine, the head of the council and elfin representative.

Next to Laymaine's painting was Ajhanon. He was dressed in the same garb as he did when I met him. Across the hall was Azize, still on his blue haze. Next to him was Derius Dracman. He had long silvery hair pulled back into a ponytail. He stood in a pinstriped black suit and was holding a cane with a large deep red orb on top. Across from him was a hobgoblin named Dorgrim Kek. He stood taller than the throne. His head and face was hidden underneath a black traveling cloak. The cloak looked to be made of cloth but shadows even as a painting. Fate said he was the representative for halflings.

Next to him was a portrait of Mr. Benjamin. He said that the image made him look fat. He was the representative for magic users like witches, wizards, and mages. Across from him was a woman sitting on the throne, legs crossed. She had a conch shell in her green hair. Fate said her name was Aquila; she was the underwater representative for the magic beneath the waves.

After her, there was a thin man dressed in a black suit with a white collar. He resembled a priest, yet his arm was bound above the elbow with leather belts. Everything from the belt to his fingers was rotted. There was a bite taken out of the meat of his hand. Even his bone was showing in some places. He wore a black goalie mask with screws holding it into his flesh. He was the undead representative. The last painting was just the golden throne.

"It was your grandfather's, but he passed away. So for now it's vacant."

At the end of the hall were two doors with a large tree etched into the wood. As we approached it, Fate said, "This is Yggdrasil. In Norse mythology, it is said to hold the realms together. The council had this put here to remind us all that we are keeping the peace between magical and non-magical beings."

After he finished speaking, he pushed the doors open, revealing a great hall. The only thing occupying it was twelve chairs against the far wall slightly covered by a desk running the length of the hall. It was set on a dais, so that those who sat in their seats could look down to the floor.

Four seats were occupied; Chancellor Laymaine sat in the sixth chair. On her left in the fifth was Arin, dressed in a white suit. In the first on the left sat Darius Dracman, and at the far end in the twelfth seat was Gruff.

Laymaine cleared her throat then said, "All who are present must be seen. In the name of the High Lord, deception will be dispelled in this hearing."

At that point, Ajhanon stepped from behind the ninth chair and sat in it, straightening his robes. Laymaine said, "Now then, as High Chancellor of the Council of Antiquities, I would like to formally welcome you to Subterra. Any questions you have will be answered at the end of the proceedings. Alexander Gates wishes to take the position of Keeper of Gatesholm. We of the council will have to approve this, so we shall vote on this issue. Who here vote for the appointment will show your hand please."

Everyone raised their hand except Darius Dracman. Chancellor Laymaine then said, "Those opposed, show your hands now."

Darius raised his hand with a stern look on his face.

Then Chancellor Laymaine said, "Appointment approved. Congratulations, Alexander."

She stamped a few papers then said, "Next order of business. Arin of the dragons has a complaint to file. Representative Arin, the floor is yours."

Arin stood up and said, "This morning, at approximately seven thirty, a dragon was taken with force by a thunder of forty dark dragons. Who ordered this act is unknown at this time. The dragon was recovered before any harm was done. The act in question is a violation and an act of war. We wish this incident be placed on record for future reference. If anyone has any information, it should be relayed to me. My thunder will take more aggressive action if another incident occurs. Thank you for the council's time."

Arin straitened his white suit and sat down. Laymaine stamped the paper in front of her and flipped it over, saying, "Arin, your complaint has been recorded in the archive. At this time, I will dismiss Mr. Gates unless he has any questions." She looked over her glasses at me.

I shrugged and said, "I have no questions at this point. Thank you for your time."

Laymaine gave a quick smile then said, "The council will take a recess and then reconvene in one human hour."

CHAPTER 22

Rose's Tea Party

FATE closed the oak doors behind me and Jaynes. We walked down the hall of portraits. We were halfway down the hall when Arin's portrait started whispering, "Hey, boys, come this way." The painted Arin was gesturing with his arms.

Jaynes walked over to the painting and touched it. His hand went through like a curtain. The canvas rippled away, revealing a passageway with a spiraling staircase. Jaynes was in the lead as we walked up the stairs. The walls were melted through. I guessed that it was one solid glass tower until a dragon blazed this staircase. It felt like walking inside a frosted glass bottle; light filtered in, but I couldn't see out.

Finally, the stairs ended to a flattened round room. There were three huge doors, all of frosted glass with silver handles. To the left of the doors was a huge window the size of Arin's dragon form. We stood in the middle of the room looking out, when we heard hard shoes behind the middle of the three doors. It opened with the sound of muffled scraping. When the door was halfway open, Rose came running out wearing a jean jumper and a pink shirt underneath. She wrapped her arms around my waist, looked up into my eyes, and said, "Mr. Alex, I am so happy to see you. Daddy said you would come."

"Of that I had no doubt. Alexander seems to be very dependable," said a voice from the doorway.

I looked up to see Arin leaning against the frame with a smile. His face had four red welts running across his cheek. "Rose has been waiting for you, haven't you?"

Rose jumped up and down repeatedly, saying yes with every jump. Rose stopped jumping and asked, "Would you come play 'tea party' with me?"

Before I could answer, she grabbed my hand and pulled me past Arin. He smiled as we went through the doorway. We hurried down another melted passage into a room with toys strewn about a plush pastel rug. She led me to a small table in the corner surround by four child-sized chairs. Pushing me into one, she darted to a wall where the bookshelf had a teapot steaming on a tray surround by small mugs. She picked it up and carefully brought it to the table. Rose set it down, and the cups slid together, making a chiming sound. She handed me a mug then set one at the other three chairs. When Arin and Jaynes came into the room, she turned and asked them to join us. They took seats across from each other, leaving the chair across from me empty. She then started to fill every cup with the steamy tea. When she was done, she said, "Oh, I forgot the milk and sugar." She set the teapot on the tray and ran out of the room.

Jaynes asked Arin, "So what happened this morning with the dark dragons?"

Arin took a deep breath then said, "They slipped into the mound just before sunrise. The dark dragon killed two watchmen stationed so Scar could catch his breakfast. Rose was playing just outside the mansion near the pool of souls. One dark dragon poisoned her with venom, but she was resistant to it. So it put her to sleep instead of killing her. I caught up with them just as they took flight. That's when the rest of their force jumped me in the sky. I fought them off with the help of Scar who saw me in the sky. By then, the four with her in their mouth had reached the outskirts of the grounds. When we reached them, they had landed in a clearing near the Erie River. Scar and I dispatched them quickly and flew her here."

I asked, "Why didn't they keep going? It would only make sense to keep moving."

Arin shifted in his seat then said, "I believe they were waiting for someone to take her off their hands, but we got there before the exchange. I know Darius Dracman had something to do with it, but I have no proof to accuse him in council."

Arin started to say something else, but the sound of Rose's hurried steps from the hall made him cut it short. The door swung open, and Rose came running in to Arin, hiding behind him. "What is wrong my little one?" Arin asked in a soothing tone.

Rose didn't say a word but pointed to the door. We all looked up to see Darius Dracman holding a glass tray of milk and sugar. He smiled a sinister smile and said, "I came to tell you the council is reconvening. I asked Rose where you were, and she dropped this tray. I did not mean to scare her. Here, Rose, you forgot this in your haste."

The words slithered out of his mouth. It sounded like a snake talking to a shaken mouse.

Arin rose from where he sat and walked over, taking the tray from Darius. Then he whispered something to him that caused Darius to bare his silver fangs and say, "But you have no proof to these false allegations. You can stop the tough-guy act, dragon. If I wanted her, I would simply have taken her. I have no need to use such lowly creatures to do my bidding."

"If I find your hand in any of this, I will strike you down where you stand," Arin said as the back of his neck started to sparkle like his silver scales. "I think you better leave before old instincts awaken."

Darius's smile widened, and he took a step forward. Then a hand grabbed his shoulder from outside the door, and he spun around. Chancellor Laymaine spoke before he completed his turn. "Yes, Darius, it is time to leave. I wish to speak with Alexander and Jaynes before the meeting."

Darius's smile faded. From where I sat, I could see him tighten his jaw. He shouldered past her and disappeared down the hall. Laymaine clapped her hands together saying, "So how are we doing? Are you two enjoying your first visit to Crystal Citadel? Oh, are we having tea? May I join your party, Rose?"

Rose spoke first, saying in an excited voice, "You sure can, Mrs. Laymaine, but I only have four chairs."

Laymaine smiled and said, "Tut-tut, child, we shall see what I can do to remedy that."

She walked over and touched Rose's chair with her left hand, causing the chair to glow in a golden light. She closed her eyes and mumbled a line of incoherent words. Then she extended her right arm. She spoke the word facsimile that caused the golden light to slide off the chair. It slid beneath the palm of her right hand and faded to another chair the same size. Laymaine sat in the newly formed chair in between Jaynes and me. Rose brought another mug and the teapot over.

Laymaine looked at Rose and said, "You are a good hostess. You have learned well from your mother."

Rose smiled and said, "The triplets taught me how to make tea."

Laymaine scooped two spoonfuls of sugar into her mug, stirred it, and took a sip. She set her mug down and said, "This is very good tea – black tea, if I am correct."

Rose's smile grew bigger. She started to rock on her heels and said, "Yes, you're correct."

Laymaine smiled and said to Arin, "You have a talented young lady on your hands."

Rose put the teapot back on the bookshelf. She then took her seat, sipping her sugar-filled tea.

CHAPTER 23

Preparations

AFTER the tea party, Arin, Rose, and Laymaine walked Jaynes and me to the large glass window in the center of the tower. "How are you boys getting home?" Laymaine asked.

I shrugged my shoulders and said, "I had not thought about it."

Then Arin said, "Well, Scar is taking Rose home. I am sure he would not mind two extra passengers."

Just then, a man walked through one of the doors and said, "Sure, we all are going to the same place, anyway. The more the merrier." The man was dressed in an all-black suit and shirt. I did a double take; he looked exactly like Arin, except for a long scar running down the right side of his face.

The man must have noticed me staring because he chuckled and said, "Yes, Arin and I are twins. We took opposite elements at birth. He is affiliated with the light, and I the dark."

Rose asked the man, "Uncle Scar, is we going home soon? I am hungry."

It all set in. This was the guardian whose features floated disturbingly in the cave. Scar responded to Rose, "We have to wait for our Keeper to finish speaking with Mrs. Laymaine. Why don't you come with me? We will see what I can find to satisfy your little tummy."

Scar and Rose went into one of the rooms, leaving the four of us alone. Laymaine waited until the door closed before she said, "The protective barrier over Gatesholm is weakened. You need to go and solidify your claim to the nexus before the morning sun rises. Otherwise, the barrier will disperse, and the whole of the world will be able to enter. It seems as if Darius Dracman has something against you. Take care in whom you choose to let in – not all are what they seem."

Arin looked at me and said, "When Scar and I found Rose, I could smell Lucius lurking about in the shadows. But when we searched for him, he bolted away. If the vampires want the nexus, then there is something more going on than we know."

"What does having ownership of the nexus mean, anyway?" I asked.

Arin started to say something when Laymaine put her hand up and said, "I will explain. Magic is what we call the use of manna. Manna runs through the world in ley lines. Like power lines conduct electricity, ley lines conduct manna. Dregus is the embodiment of said manna. He keeps the ley lines flowing properly. If he were to fail at his job, the lines could cause an explosion greater than any bomb constructed. The resulting blast would destroy the world."

"Manna is not good, nor is it evil. It is neutral. Like everything else, it is its misuse we concern ourselves with. Your grandfather took it upon himself to defend Dregus. He built your house as a stronghold against any who would misuse this well of power. Magical ownership has been the strongest ward against that. Now you have inherited his land, which makes you the new protector – dubbed the Keeper."

Laymaine finished; her words weighed heavily on my mind. Jaynes – seeing the strain on my face – said, "Don't worry, Lexxy. I will help you."

Arin looked at Jaynes and said, "Only Alexander can bear this burden. All you can do is support him."

Scar came back with Rose in tow. Rose had a huge red sucker in her hand and an even bigger smile on her face.

Chancellor Laymaine said, "I have some things to take care of before the council reconvenes. Boys, you have a good flight home, and Arin will see you in a few minutes." Then she opened a door and disappeared down the spiral stairs.

After she left, Scar said, "So I take it we are ready to go? Well, I guess I should change then."

Arin said, "Step to the wall."

He moved so his back was against a wall. Rose, Jaynes, and I joined him while Scar remained in the center of the room.

Scar let out long screech, and his clothes turned into a thick black smoke. The cloud expanded and grew until the whole room was engulfed, aside from the narrow perimeter in which we stood. A black light flashed then the smoke was gone, leaving a black dragon standing in the middle of the room. Scar turned his huge head to face us; a purple patch was visible on his right jaw.

"All aboard," he said with the startling grin.

Jaynes and I climbed onto his serpentine neck. Rose stamped her feet and said, "I want to fly, Daddy. Can't I fly?"

Scar shook his head, causing us to lie flat against the back of his head. He said, "You can fly if you can keep up. There will be no stopping to rest."

Rose smiled and jumped with excitement. She said, "I am a big girl. I can do it, Uncle Scar." Rose let out a screech. Her pink cloud covered her little body. Soon she was in her dragon form.

Scar said, "OK, here we go." He unfolded his wings and looked out of the huge window. With a lunge, he jumped into the glass. Instead of shattering the window, it made a sound like water dropping into a puddle.

CHAPTER 24

Flying Home

IN an instant, we went flying out of Niagara Falls with a splash. The sun blinded me as my eyes got used to the change in light. A moment later, I heard another splash, and the little pink dragon came soaring up next to Scar. I looked back at the giant waterfall flowing majestically into its plunge pool beneath. From there, we flew down the river, passing the whirlpool called the Devil's Hole. Then the two dragons turned in and flew high over the city of Buffalo. The tall buildings of downtown blurred into a sprawling grid of houses. After a half hour, the houses disappeared into a thicket of trees. They descended lower and lower until my home finally came into view. We flew past the house to the rocky structure, and then swooped into their bowl-shaped den.

Scar landed in the field with a thud, causing rocks to jump off the ground. Rose came swooping after him, but her landing was more of a sliding crash. Dust blew up as she slid on her belly, coming to a stop as I climbed off Scar's massive neck.

Ladonna came running out of the entrance cave where Scar usually stood guard. She dashed over to Rose, scooping her up with inhuman strength. She smothered her dragon head in human kisses. I could see Rose's tail thrashing about in the dirt as she struggled from her mother's grip. Ladonna let her go. Turning on her heels, she walked over to where we stood.

Scar – who had already returned to his human form – walked over, smoothing his black suit. "All is well here, I trust. Then, my lady, if you would excuse me. There is a need to find two young ones to train as guard for when I leave my post. Ladies and gentlemen, I shall leave you to your own devices." Scar bowed to Ladonna, then turned and walked into the entrance cave.

During our exchange, Rose had also changed into her human form. She came skipping over and grabbed Ladonna's arm. She hugged it tightly like her teddy at night. Ladonna looked down at Rose and smiled affectionately. She then said, "Those girls came by while you were gone. They were upset when I would not let them wait in the house. The one told me to have you call her when you got back." She looked up from Rose and looked into my eyes. "I already warned you about them."

I responded by saying, "I trust her, but thank you for your advice."

Brushing off her concern once again, Jaynes grabbed my shoulder and said, "I'm heading to the house." Then he started walking toward the entrance tunnel.

Rose said, "Bye, Mr. Jaynes. Come by and play sometime. Mommy, I am hungry. Uncle Scar gave me some venison, but it was only a little one." She pulled on her mother's arm as she spoke.

"What has happened to our manners? Yes, we will go home now. This is where we part, Alexander. Do not be a stranger in our den. You are more than welcome to visit anytime," Ladonna said. Afterward, she and Rose disappeared into the woods toward their mansion behind the waterfall.

On the way to the house, I had the feeling of being followed. Every time I turned to look, nothing was out of the ordinary. I passed by Dante's church when I heard growling coming from a clump of bushes. I stopped and stared in the direction, when something sprang out. It looked like a lizard the size of a horse. It looked like a crocodile but had six legs and a row of razor spikes on its back. It charged at me, tongue licking the air.

I turned and ran as fast as I could. I could hear it behind me, tearing through the undergrowth with ease, hissing and growling as it chased me. Its feet made loud thuds as they pushed the creature on. As I came into the backyard, I could hear Dregus in my head saying "Faster, we are ready for that thing." I came running around the porch, and out the corner of my eye, I saw Jaynes leap off the porch holding a sword. He landed on its snot and drove the sword through its skull. The blade went all the way through into the ground beneath. The beast thrashed about for a second then went limp.

Jaynes stood astride the body, breathing heavily. He released the hilt of the sword, and it turned to dust in the wind. He stepped over the carcass carefully and walked over to me. He grabbed my shoulders and spun me around saying, "Doesn't look like it got you. You must have been hauling ass."

He laughed as he walked back over to the dead lizard, kicking it as he spoke, "If this thing would have bit you, any number of things could have happened. Their saliva has multiple uses. Grandpa used it to make sleeping tonic or to paralyze things. He told me once that they are deadly even to most dragons. Why was it chasing you?"

Just then, Dante and six wolves came running from the side of the house. He came to a stop in full view of the dead threat. "My lord, that was a good kill, Jaynes," he said, out of breath. "I saw this hellish thing tracking you when you walked by, Keeper. Its eyes had a purple glow about them when we came out behind it. The damned thing turned invisible – never seen a Razier do that."

As he spoke, the wolves all dragged the Razier's body away from the house.

I stood there mortified; this thing was the same one from Allegany. I asked Dregus in my head, "Did this Razier follow me here?"

Dregus responded, "If it had, I would not be as concerned. I fear there is something else amiss here." Then he went silent once again.

"What is going on?" Dante asked. "First the little dragon, now this Razier? I know something was controlling the Razier for sure. Their eyes don't do that, and they can't turn invisible," he said, sidestepping the crimson ground where the Razier was slain. "Well, I'm going to patrol the grounds. I'll keep you posted."

Dante turned and jogged in the direction the wolves went. Jaynes walked to the front door saying, "Buttons wants to talk to you. He is in the kitchen."

The door closed behind him. I stared toward the porch when a black sedan pulled up the driveway. I stood at the foot of the stairs as the car pulled up.

CHAPTER 25

Ownership Conclusion

THE door swung open, and Laymaine stepped out of the car. She wore a woven hat with a floral summer dress. She walked up to me with a smile and said, "I see that your yard looks as good as when your grandfather cared for it. I see the roses have not bloomed yet. Do send me a bouquet when they do. Zavies's flowers were always better than those in any flower shop, though that is not the reason for my visit. I have to ensure the security of the vortex. Speaking of which, how is Dregus these days?" She removed her hat; her red hair was tied in a bun atop her head. She walked over and wrapped her hands around me in a friendly embrace.

I said, "Drogues is doing well."

Jaynes opened the door, saying, "Buttons said there was somebody coming, but I see you know that already."

Suddenly the birdfeeder glowed brightly. Sabrina burst out of the brush beneath it. She zipped over to Laymaine, who extended her hand and allowed the fairy to land. The fairy pinched the bottom of her dress and curtsied. She raised herself and said, "Greetings, Lady Laymaine. I would like to welcome you to Gatesholm. I hope your visit is a pleasurable one. As you can see, we have tended to the grounds as you have instructed. I hope you're pleased with our work, my queen."

Laymaine nodded her head, saying, "I am pleased with what I have of seen so far. Keep up the good work. How is the vegetable garden?"

The fairy bowed her head and said, "We have cleaned the rotten plants, yet the new growth has yet to take root."

Laymaine smiled then said, "That is fine, all things take time. Continue your diligence, and you will be rewarded."

The fairy curtsied again saying "Yes, my lady" then took flight, heading to the left side of the house.

"Alexander, would you escort me to the vortex? We have to finalize your ownership of the land to conclude the contract." She walked past me as Jaynes held the door for her. I went in after her while Jaynes closed and locked the door.

Laymaine stood in the living room, looking around. I said to her, "I know the vortex is supposed to be underneath the house. Also, something about it is important to magic, so it has to be protected."

She smiled and said, "Alexander, all your questions will be answered downstairs. Have you been inside your basement yet?"

I shook my head from side to side.

She then said, "Well, why don't you lead the way."

I walked to the basement door; its padlock hung dust-covered. Laymaine came behind me and said, "Touch the lock, it requires no key."

I did as she said, grabbing the lock as if I was going to unlock it. The lock clicked in my hand, and I pulled it out of the hole. The weight of the lock was heavy in my hand, so I slid it into my pocket.

A gust of cold air burst forth as I opened the door. Laymaine put both her hands on her dress to keep it down. When the gust stopped, I walked down the spiral staircase. The cinder-block walls became increasingly wetter as I descended further until I reached a torch-lit circular room with an arched doorway close to the last step. Through the archway and down a well-lit hall I led the way. The walls had scrolling lines in looping patterns. Laymaine's heeled footsteps echoed behind me. At the end of the hall, I came to an iron door. It was etched in the same scrolling lines. I opened the door with ease and walked through into a large domed room.

Two steps into the room, I heard Laymaine clear her throat. I turned to see her standing just before the doorway. She looked at me and said, "I, High Chancellor Laymaine, formally request entry from the Keeper of Gatesholm." Her voice bounced around the empty room.

She nodded her head at me, so I said, "Mrs. Laymaine, of course you can. Aren't you already inside?"

Out of nowhere, a strong gust of wind blew past me, the force of which made me stumble forward. From behind me, Dregus's voice said, "Alexander, you still have much to discover and learn."

I turned slowly as Laymaine walked past me.

Dregus was standing with his arms crossed in the center of the room. Laymaine said, "Dregus, it has been too long since we last saw each other. I hope you have been well." She walked over to Dregus, and they embraced each other. "We must save our greetings for later, because Alexander has to complete his ownership. So come forward, Keeper, and claim your birthright."

My legs started to shake as I moved closer. It felt like trying to keep balance during an earthquake. I looked around the room, and dust puffed out between the bricks. Then I noticed the room was shaking as I went further toward the center. The air behind Ladonna and Dregus began to swirl; it looked like a tornado from the top. Then from the eye of the storm, I could see a bird soaring toward me. By the time I made it to Dregus and Ladonna, I could make out details. The wings touched the sides of the tunnel; the head was human. I realized it wasn't a bird but a dark-haired man with golden wings on his back.

The man flew out of the vortex, landing in our little group. His wings folded to his back, he opened his arms and said, "Friends, I have not seen each of you since the original induction. I see the next Keeper has come of age. My time is short, so let us begin. Let's join hands."

He reached out and grasped Dregus's and Laymaine's hands. They extended their free arms toward me.

When I completed the circle, the winged man started speaking again. "To the High Lord, thank you for allowing us to gather here. This young man is Alexander Gates. He wishes to safeguard the manna vortex. As his fathers have done before him, he is pure of heart, my lord. Grant his wish of Keeper of Gatesholm. Allow him to learn greatly and live long. In your name we give our gratitude, Amen."

The man looked me; he started to cry tears of blood. Then his eyes rolled to white. A voice that was not his own spoke out of his mouth in a language I never heard, but I understood every word, "Alexander Gates, I grant your wishes. Be humble in your duties, patient with those around you. Be fair and benevolent in your decisions. Now go forth in peace."

The man began to convulse uncontrollably as soon as the voice stopped. Then I began to shake as well.

CHAPTER 26

Hidden Truths

THE next thing I knew, I was sitting inside Dregus's study in a soft armchair. My head was pounding as I looked around. Across from me, Laymaine was talking in low tones with the winged man. Dregus was at the fireplace pulling off a whistling teapot. He turned around and said, "Our Keeper has awakened, and faster than Zavies did."

I asked, "What happened?"

Laymaine answered me. "The High Lord blessings are not easily obtained. His exiting the circle seems to cause your blackout."

I looked at the winged man, asking him, "Who are you, and where did you come from?"

The man smiled and said, "I am the Metatron – the voice of the High Lord. I came from the kingdom of light."

I looked from Laymaine to Dregus in bewilderment.

Metatron spoke again, "Let me explain. In the beginning, darkness ruled this existence. Then the light lord came into this plane. Do you believe in God, Alexander? I only ask this because I think your grandfather would have read you the tales and taught you the lessons. I am sure you have gathered in a place of worship.

"Here is the truth, of which has been expunged from that book. Those who remember are few, so hear me well. You know of the story of the Garden of Eden. If only reality were so simple! Before there banishment, those humans were part of the chain of light, immortal and free of the knowledge we now call commonplace. Their world consisted of a highland that seemed to be made of light. The outer edge of which was their garden and the golden gates. After that was a valley leading to the gates of the Dark Realm. This – in contrast – consumed light, letting none escape.

"The High Lord, who remains unnamed, reigns for all time in Highland. His personal guard acted as marshalls throughout reality. Creatures who create and nurture life resided in the Highland. The Dark Realm is where the creatures of destruction and chaos dwell. Creatures that consume and devour flesh, those who contort or gain power from souls. These existed for eons without disruption. There was a war between the high guards. It started by one who was corrupted by the High Lord's opposite. Skip forward some years, after his banishment from the Highland.

"The corrupted ones slithered in secretly and coaxed man into disobedience. This was the cause of crafted couple's banishment. Being compassionate, the High Lord would not dispatch them into the Dark Realm, where his artwork would become food or worse. So he ripped a hole in the valley between the two gates. In the center of the valley, he placed a new realm.

"The High Lord filled this middle land with a life circle and sent the two into the circle. So they would not be alone, he allowed magic entrance as well. Man could not return to the Highland, but magic could. For magic was not condemned to the middle land. When man learned that magic could do what he could not, they became envious and jealous of magic. Coveting the ability, man began attempting to gain that power. Yet when something is unknown, it is difficult to grasp the way to use it properly.

"The Middle Age was an example of humans trying to comprehend magic. Some tried to learn the ways of magic. Yet when those who were in power found out magic users, they were put to death. This was on a grand scale that, even being accused of magic use, you were tortured into confessing. Most would say they were users just to stop the pain.

"Humanity is closer now more than ever to understanding with science. Your ability to quantify molecules is the first step at best. Magic is a higher form of science – that's the simplest way too explain it. Where science manipulates the world physically, magic does it mentally. Doing such requires more usage of the brain at one time than humans have currently. While some humans have the potential, as a race, you have a lot more to evolve."

Dregus walked over and handed me a mug smelling of coffee. Then he turned and gave one to the Metatron then said, "I think that is enough history for today. How about some current events? Alexander was attacked recently by one of those vile tracking lizards – also, the kidnapping of a dragon adolescent by dark dragons."

Ladonna said, "I was not aware of a Razer attack."

The Metatron's face went from joyful to concerned. He shook his head, saying, "We have been receiving reports of these kinds of events. Creatures that were bound were coming unshackled or traversing the dimensional gate – coming to earth causing trouble. Some believe that *he* is trying to return, and these events are part of his emergence. Yet the High Lord still remains silent on this matter."

"If *his* return is imminent, light will need a stronghold. If you agree, Alexander, we will reinforce your land's protective wards against the darkness," the Metatron finished as I glanced over to Dregus. He was lightly sipping his tea.

Dregus's eyes looked over his mug and blinked purposely, then returned to what is inside his mug. Returning my gaze to the Metatron, I said, "Yes, I think more protection would help rather than be a hindrance."

The Metatron looked me in my eyes and said, "It is settled then." Then he rose to his feet and shook his shoulders. As his wings unfolded, I heard Dregus set his mug down. Then the Metatron clapped his hands together.

CHAPTER 27

Extra Protection

IN my next blink, I felt the chair slide from underneath me. The bookshelves around me shifted into the stone walls of the vortex room. I fell onto the cold hard floor as the mug I was holding shattered into a mix of dark tea and porcelain chips.

Dregus reach down saying, "That was one of my favorite mugs. Oh well, I'll repair it later. Let me help you up."

The Metatron watch silently as Dregus pulled me up with a jerk of his arm. Once I was standing, Metatron said, "Once I leave, the protection granted to your land will be increased a billionfold. All you have contracted will be anointed and divinely blessed. Only those you deem worthy can enter or leave, all will be subject to your will and judgment. In addition, your touch can heal any wound, toxin, curse, or disease. These abilities we grant to you only on this land. Walk in peace, Alexander, and leave prints of the same."

The Metatron leapt into the air toward the ceiling. Then doing a loop, it whooshed into the vortex. The room shook with the sonic boom that closed the vortex.

The room went quiet, the door swung open, and Ladonna stood there with her hands on her hips. "Alexander, will you see me to my car? We can leave Dregus to do some chores in his study."

Ladonna and I conversed about the Razer until we were underneath the starry night sky. She gave me a maternal kiss on my cheek as I opened her car door. Once inside, she looked at me and said, "Your grandfather would be proud of the man you are becoming. Have a good night, Keeper of Gatesholm. Until we next meet." Then she drove off in a cloud of dust.

I walked up and sat on the stairs of the porch. I could hear voices and laughter coming from the side of the house. A few moments later Jaynes and Dante came walking out. Jaynes looked as if he had too many to drink. He staggered even while being held up by his shoulder. "Our patrols found him near the lake with an empty bottle of Jack Daniels." Dante started to say before Jaynes slurred out "that mere-bitch finished the bottle and then swam away. I have half a mind to swim down there and give her a piece of my mind. Doesn't she know who I am; I'm the Keeper's keeper." Jaynes stumbled off of Dante and over to me. He fell onto the pouch wrapped his arm around my neck saying "Lexxy, tell Wolfman who I am!" I shook my head and said "thanks Dante for bringing him home."

Dante and I conversed for a while about the wolf hunting-party's reports. He said all was quiet and the hunt was plentiful. All the while, Jaynes muttered to himself to sleep in the swing.

Dante departed saying, "I got to get back before the meat gets cold. The natives told me to thank you for the extra protection. They will all sleep easy from now on knowing you're here. Zavies set up a good plan, I have to say. You are definitely all he said you would be and more. Goodnight, Keeper." Then he walked off around the house.

I went over to Jaynes and shook him. He swung his arm at an attempt at stopping this assault on his dreams, so I left him to his drinking slumber and went in the house. I made my way up the stairs to the third floor, through the study into Grandpa's old room. When I entered, I was shocked. The room was now furnished with the things from my room on the second floor. Everything was in where it had been down there.

I backed out and dashed down to find an empty space – walls bare, floors polished to a reflective shine.

Dregus's voice spoke, "The house has accepted you as the landlord. It took the previous owner's things and filed them away in the library. Your belongings were then moved into the master bedroom. There is more to tell you, but for now, go get some rest. Good night, Keeper."

Dregus's voice faded from my mind, so I returned to the master bedroom. Falling into my pillow, sleep overtook me before I even noticed.

CHAPTER 28

The Stone Golem

I AWOKE suddenly by a low windy voice calling my name. I slid out of the bed and walked throughout the house. Everywhere I went, I couldn't tell where it was coming from. In the master bedroom, the voice echoed from downstairs. On the second floor, I felt sandwiched by its drone. In the kitchen, the voice came from both the living room and the stairway I had just descended. Feeling frustration after checking the vortex room to no avail, I yelled out loud, "Where are you? Show yourself!"

The house shook violently, as if in a hurricane.

Dust filled the air and floorboards creaked above me. Then the voice called out, "I am all around you." Feeling uneasy, I thought the house was talking. I laughed at the thought until the house shook again with the voice "yes!" in my head. I contacted Dregus, yet he didn't respond. Then the house shook once again. The voice followed with "It is only you and us."

I started to feel overwhelmed. Trying to sound confident, I spoke, "Who are you?"

The disembodied voice responded, "We are the oaken ones. Our forms were used to shape this house. We are now the mind of this structure. We welcome you with this gift."

I was bombarded with the flashes of a vision: first of my grandfather standing in a clearing with four great oak trees surrounding him. As my grandfather began speaking to the trees, they twisted into each other. The four became one, they following the continued instructing. Soon he was standing in the living room. The vision faded, and I found myself in the same spot.

The voice spoke again, "Now you are the Keeper. Your word is ours to follow. We know all that goes on here. We remember all that has occurred. What is ours is yours to use."

Then my body started to shake as the house did. The room faded away.

I could feel hands on my upper arms shaking me. "Lexxy, wake up. The girls are here." Jaynes's voice sounded distant as the shaking continued.

I opened my eyes slowly; Jaynes was standing over me. He shook me again saying "wake up."

I batted at his arms. "I'm up, I'm up. Stop it, Jaynes. What's going on?"

Jaynes released me and stepped back. "The girls called. They said the gate won't open," he said.

I wiped the sleep out of my eyes saying, "Well, why not let them in?" I slid out of the bed, put on a shirt and my shoes, and walked downstairs. Jaynes followed after me.

I opened the front door and started down the driveway. Before I made it around the bend, the girls pulled up. Nevalin jumped from the passenger side and almost tackled Jaynes off his feet. Ontia got out, saying as she walked, "The gate wouldn't open when Nevalin pulled at it. When she got back into the car, it swung open. That was weird." She walked over and planted a long kiss on my lips and smiled as she pulled away.

Nevalin said, "It's going to be hot today. Jaynes told me that you have a lake we could swim in."

Ontia let out a sigh and said, "That's why we came. Please, baby, can we go swimming?"

"Sure, we all can go," I said, looking at Jaynes.

After parking the car, we walked through the forest to the lake. The air seemed calm as we arrived. The girls stripped off their clothes down to their bikinis underneath. They both dashed into the water, splashing all the way. We swam and played in the cool water until the sun started to go down. That was when Ontia said something about going to grab a bite to eat. So we collected our clothes from the ground and headed back to the house.

Just before the car came into view, we heard the sound of glass shattering. We hurried our step to find a huge pile of rocks on top of her car. Ontia screamed, "My car! What happened to my car!" She ran over to examine the damage. The rock pile extended from the ground in front to the roof. The front windshield had shattered into the car.

Ontia went to push the rocks to see if she could move them. When she touched the rocks, she jumped back yelling, "It moved."

As she said that, the stones moved. They shifted from the roof in the form of an arm and a hand that made a grab at Ontia, of which she jumped back further to avoid. The stones shifted off the car.

I watched as the rock pile gathered into a humanoid form. The top resembled a head with red eyes looking out through a shadowy spot. I heard a voice that sounded like rocks falling say "Dark blood no allowed." The creature took three steps toward Ontia in another attempt to grab her. This time she ducked as the stone hands clapped together. Splinters of rock and dust fell on her as she rolled away on the ground.

When the stone creature noticed her a few feet away, it took another step toward her. Stretching out its massive arm, it tried to smash Ontia with a vertical smack. The ground shook as Ontia skipped away, narrowly missing the creature's hand. Jaynes dropped down on one knee and placed the top of his fist on the ground. He stood up and charged at the stone giant with his earthen sword over his shoulder. He shouted a war cry as he swung the sword at the creature. The giant raised its arm in defense as Jaynes sunk the blade into its arm. The golem yanked its arm back, and the sword was ripped from Jaynes's hands – the force of which knocked Jaynes to the ground. With its other arm, the creature made a move to smash Jaynes into pulp.

CHAPTER 29

Secrets Revealed

AT this point, Sabrina burst forth from the bird feeder. Tears streamed down her face as she flew toward the fray yelling "don't hurt him!" She darted past me and landed on the stone creature's raised hand. "Eric, stop this right now!"

The stone golem froze, its arm stretched over Jaynes.

"Keeper, I'm sorry. He was just doing his job."

I raised my eyebrows and said, "Attacking my brother is his job? How is that a job description? After all that's happened to me, he could be some bad minion sent to kill me."

Sabrina crossed her tiny arms, pouted her lips, and stamped her foot. "Eric is my friend. He wouldn't hurt someone unless they're bad for the land. Eric, at ease."

The stone golem lowered its arm and sat on the ground. Legs crossed and his fists pressed together, knuckle to knuckle.

Sabrina fluttered around him during the whole move. She settled on the golem saying, "See he will follow your orders and anyone you have contracted. Otherwise, he will attack anything he sees as a threat to the land."

During this display, Jaynes and Ontia had retreated behind me. "How are they threatening the land?"

Sabrina threw her hands up while shrugging. "How should I know? Ask him!" she said.

So I shifted my gaze to the golem saying, "Eric, what is the threat you see?"

Eric raised his hand, pointed at me, and said, "Dark-blood girls."

I spun on my heels and looked at Ontia and Nevalin. Ontia stood with her arms crossed while Nevalin cowered behind her. "My lady, what shall we do?" Nevalin asked.

Ontia stepped forward saying, "Yes. I am of dark blood, but I mean you no harm, Alexander. I have had many opportunities, as you know. My father and brother know nothing of our relationship, and I aim to keep it as such."

"Who is your father?" Jaynes asked.

I shook my head, answering his question, "Darius Dracman. You're the daughter no one knows."

Ontia shook her head yes, not losing her prideful posture. "I was fully aware of who you were when we first met in class. Zavies sent me to you. It was of his design that we are having this conversation. Your grandfather, Jaynes Matthew Gates, was a shaper. His magical name, Zavies, was given to him because of his gift. It's rare to possess the ability to shape the world around you. It was fabled even in the light land."

She paused as if thinking, then continued, "A few months before your grandfather came to me. My father started meeting with a man named Necros. From the first time I met him, I could tell he was pure evil. Even now, his evil intent poisons my father's mind. Necros has twisted him into a lapdog. Everything out of my father's mouth is 'my lord this' and 'Lord Necros that.' My father is the reason for all your trouble. If I'm any good judge of character, Necros is only going to make things worse."

Ontia stopped speaking. It was quiet for a moment when I said, "Eric, return to your watch. Sabrina, thank you for your help! Ontia, I think we should continue this inside."

Sabrina smiled and fluttered off to the bird feeder, while Eric stood up and stamped off into the forest. As I turned to walk into the house, Dregus telepathically said, "A wise decision, Keeper. I shall meet you in the living room."

CHAPTER 30

My First Contract

WHEN we entered the house, there was a tall, bald, chocolate-skinned man sitting in the sofa chair. He wore an emerald-green suit with his legs crossed sipping a mug of steamy tea. He set his cup down and stood up as we entered. Once we were all in, he said, "Hello, ladies. My name is Mr. Brown. I am Alexander's housing advisor. It is good to meet you in person."

I looked at the man who seemed familiar to me, yet I didn't say it out loud. Jaynes seemed to catch something I didn't; he said, "Mr. Brown, it has been a while. How have you been?"

Mr. Brown and Jaynes shook hands. Then Mr. Brown reached for mine to shake, and he said, "I think it is in our best interest to contract these ladies."

Nevalin – who had sat with Ontia on the couch – said, "I'm not signing anything I don't read first."

Ontia shook her head and said, "Let the man explain."

"Thank you, Ms. Dracman." Mr. Brown started, "If you are to be one of Alexander's allies, you must enter into a magical agreement. I am here to assist him in the context of said agreement. Alexander has yet to make a new contract."

In my head, I heard Dregus's voice say, "This is a good disguise, don't you think?" Then Mr. Brown winked at me. That's when I realized who he really was. He took a breath and continued, "First, we would require complete secrecy on any information you gain in dealing with Alexander. Also, you would need to nonexclusively disclose all information known to you. If you decide to break your word, you would be required to instantaneously meet the sun. If you have any terms or conditions to add, they would be considered."

Nevalin shifted uncomfortably in her seat.

Ontia smiled slightly. "The two of us only require a few additions to your proposal. We require proper sleeping accommodations as well as the freedom to come and go as we wish. If I am absent too long, my father will grow suspicious. Also, if a few meals could be acquired on occasion, we will agree to your terms."

Nevalin gasped and said, "My lady, I do not wish to meet the sun."

Ontia looked at her, saying, "Then we must keep our word."

Ontia smiled and looked back to Mr. Brown. Mr. Brown looked at me and asked, "Are these terms acceptable, Alexander?"

Then the attentions of the room turned to me. I thought for a minute and said, "Acquiring a meal? What does that mean?"

Ontia smiled again, saying, "We are vampire – what do you think it means?"

Jaynes crossed his arms and rolled his eyes. "Your girlfriend wants you to find her humans to kill, Lexxy."

Ontia glared at Jaynes. "No, no, I want you to find me a donor. I don't kill my donors. Killing is just wasteful and draws too much attention. How do you think I have gone undetected this long?"

"I will accept your terms as long as you don't kill anyone," I said.

Ontia then added, "I only kill those who deserve it. I have never looked lightly at ending someone's life."

Mr. Brown clapped his hands together saying, "Now that we are all in agreement, I shall take my leave. Ladies, I do hope you have a good night. Jaynes, it's always a pleasure. And to you, Alexander, I know we shall see each other real soon."

Mr. Brown turned and walked out the front door without another word. Ontia turned to me saying, "So are we OK? I know it wrong to pursue a relationship with you. Even still, I can't help that I feel what I feel."

I stood there for a moment then said, "I care for you as well. If I can get past your secret, then we will be fine. But it will take some time."

Ontia smiled, saying, "I have all of eternity to live, so you take as much time as you need. I would wait until the end of days for you, Alexander. I have to go, but I will call you in a few days to check in. I love you, Alexander."

She stood up and wrapped me in a tight embrace. She kissed me lightly on my cheek and headed for the door. Nevalin stood up said good-bye and followed Ontia out the door.

Jaynes said, "I'm going to head out too. Call me if you need anything, little brother." Then he walked out as well.

EPILOGUE

Alone in the house, I went to make something to eat. After I finished my meal, Dregus contacted me, asking me to come to his study. Once I arrived, he offered me a cup of tea. We talked about the dream I had that morning. He sat quietly listening until I finished. He then said, "Even though it was a dream, the events that it showed were real. Your grandfather was a shaper. He could create items out of nothing, or change an event to his desired outcome. His power was unlike any I have ever known. You have his spark, which is why he chose you to be the keeper. I can show you the path, but only you can walk it."

Dregus continued, "You have contracted all of those affiliated with the light. Yet this land is a safe haven for both light and dark. You contracted the creatures of the light. Therefore, you have to contract those residents who are affiliated with the darkness as well. Outside of Subterra, you are the keeper of the largest population of magic on the East Coast."

When he paused, I asked, "You mean there are other places with magical creatures?"

Dregus laughed for a moment then said, "Yes, your grandfather visited many places before finding me. Most of them exist on intersecting ley lines – some of just darkness and, adversely, some of purely light. There are even a few that are used to lock creatures away, sort of like a prison. Just as humanity is abundant, so too is magic. This land is unique not only for my presence, but for the balance your grandfather was able to achieve. Light existing in harmony with dark is a hard thing to accomplish."

Dregus paused again and took a sip from a mug that was hidden behind a stack of books. I tried to think of a question but could not come up with one. He set the mug down and started speaking again. "Before you go, I have to give you the Ruby Ring."

I asked, "Where do I have to go to get this ring – in a jewelry store?"

Dregus shook his head. "Your lack of knowledge still amuses me." He stood up and walked over to the fireplace. Inside, a fire burned quietly. "Come out and meet Alexander, Efrit," Dregus asked. The fire disappeared into the coals then blazed up, filling the chimney.

Before the flames returned to normal, a large bird burst forth. It flew around the room then landed on top of Dregus's desk. The bird looked at Dregus for a few minutes then turned its head to me. It resembled a peacock, except its feathers looked to be on fire. The air around them seemed to wave as it heated. Efrit blinked its yellow eyes then nodded its head.

Dregus said, "This is Efrit the Phoenix. He is one of the few left in the world. Most of them left during the middle age of man. He has a gift for you." Dregus opened a drawer and pulled out a golden ring. He placed it on the desk. Efrit walked over to it and picked it up in his beak. He started to hum then walked over to me. I held out my hand, and he placed the ring in my palm. Now the ring had a red jewel fastened to it. Efrit stepped back, flapping his wings.

Dregus said, "Well, put it on. This is the Ruby Ring. It holds the power of fire. With it, you will be able to bend fire to your will."

I slid the ring on my finger next to the Ring of Sight. It felt warm on my hand.

Dregus pulled a candle out of his desk and said, "Think about how you would light this candle."

I did as he instructed, imagining the wick alive with a flame. The instant the image came to mind, the candle erupted with fire that tickled the ceiling. Dregus smiled, and Efrit hopped on the desk, flapping his wings. "He seems happy with your control – as am I. You can do much more than light candles, but this was a safe way to test your control."

Efrit screeched loudly, and Dregus said, "Yes, I will tell him. He wants you to know that if you ever need him, all you have to do is point the ring and say his name. Phoenix are pure magic. Their entire being can be used in a number of ways. For example, if you were to obtain one of Efrit's feathers, it would retain its flame even if immersed in water. We could sit for hours discussing a Phoenix's various properties. We can save that lesson for another time."